WHAT GOOD MOMS DO

and

Other Stories

by

Marie Anderson

What Good Moms Do and Other Stories copyright © 2017 by Marie Anderson

This is a work of fiction. Any resemblance to actual persons, living or dead, events, or locales is entirely coincidental or used fictitiously.

All rights reserved.
ISBN-10: 154263525X
ISBN-13: 978-1542635257

*To Bob, Eric, Matt, Jane,
and Taco*

Contents

The Assignment • 1

Bad Things • 7

Barbed Wire • 14

Between Hits • 21

The Box under the Bed • 23

Change of Color • 30

A Chemical Equation • 36

Coat Check • 44

Crosswords • 58

Damaged Goods • 67

Flush • 71

A Gift from Santa • 74

Handshake of Peace • 77

Innuendoes • 84

Jee • 92

Keeping Score • 99

Lola • 103

A Matter of School Pride • 106

Mucked • 114

Next • 117

Quieting Lambent • 122

Rosa • 129

Scaredy Cat • 136

Sincerely, Emma • 141

Slaughtering the Fatted Calf • 147

Tenley's Mouse • 155

What Good Moms Do • 163

Author's Note • 177

What Good Moms Do

and

Other Stories

The Assignment
First published in *Downstate Story* (2009)

LARK HEARD THE footsteps before she saw him. She looked up from spooning strained peaches into her baby's mouth. A man peered through her open kitchen window, pressing his nose into the screen. He held up something that looked like a silver cell phone. He wore a blue shirt with an opened pack of cigarettes in the breast pocket. He was brown, the color of strong coffee.

"Read your meter," he called through the window. He smiled, and she saw that one front tooth gleamed whiter than the others.

Lark scooped Myna out of the infant seat on the table and hurried to the back door.

Ask for identification, she thought, but she found herself opening the door and letting him in, and then, the two of them facing each other in her mud room, he towering over her by at least a foot, it seemed pointless to ask. It seemed like a white suburban mom thing to ask, which is what she was.

"You want to check the ID?" he asked.

"Oh, of course not," she said.

"Of course not," he repeated, and she felt like she'd insulted him.

He looked past her, into her kitchen, his head nodding the way everyone's did when they gazed upon her kitchen's expensive simplicity. She followed his gaze, seeing afresh her gleaming white Corian counters, her smooth cherry wood cabinets, the wide-plank maple floor.

He looked at her. A frown puckered his forehead. His eyes were a green tea color, and he blinked erratically, like novice wearers of contact lenses blink.

"I got ID," he said, though he made no move to show it.

"It's fine," she said. "I know you're a meter reader." Myna squirmed in her arms.

His eyes narrowed. "That right?" He looked up at her kitchen ceiling ten feet high, the recessed lighting, the paddle fan over the kitchen table stirring the air.

"What's that saying?" he asked. "If it walk like a duck, look like a duck, then it be a duck?"

"I'm sorry?" she asked. She saw that his shoes, red Nikes, were muddy. Chunks of clay, as though he'd just come from a field, trailed behind him, a trail of dirt in her mud room that she itched to sweep away.

He sighed. "Naw. Don't be sorry. It is what it is."

He smiled again, but the smile did not give her comfort. His shoes, dear God, his shoes. The black woman who'd come the last few times had worn work boots. Her ID had hung in a laminated tag around her neck. And the breast pocket of her shirt had *Peoples Gas* stitched on it. No, not *Peoples Gas*. It was *Nicor Gas* here in the suburbs. *Peoples Gas* at their little Victorian frame in Chicago, two blocks away from a public school where nobody in that newly gentrified neighborhood dared to send their children.

It was why they'd moved after Myna was born.

The boys who attended that school were bused in, and they all wore pants like the stranger now standing in her kitchen: oversized khakis, lumpy with deep, flapped pockets up and down both legs.

Myna wriggled in her arms, and Lark's muscles tightened. Who would hurt a mother holding a baby?

Her mouth hurt from smiling.

"Beautiful," he said, looking at her.

"The kitchen?" she said quickly. "Sure, now it's OK. But it used to be four rooms. It was the ugliest kitchen in the world. It had no windows."

"Sound like my kitchen," he said.

He wasn't exactly bald. Black hair fuzzed his head, wispy and fragile, like her little brother's had been after the chemotherapy. Her only sibling. He'd died the day he'd received his acceptance letter from Notre Dame. Tall and thin like the meter reader. The first from their South Side parish to make it into the prestigious university. They'd buried him with the acceptance letter tucked in his pocket.

"Well, I'll show you down to the basement," she said. "The meter's hard to spot. It's pretty much buried behind some shelving."

He followed her down the basement stairs. Her shoulders stiffened, ready for a blow from the silver object he carried, the thing that supposedly read meters.

She turned on lights, led him through the laundry room and into the back of the basement. She stopped by her husband's workbench and glanced at Jay's claw hammer on the workbench. If she hadn't been carrying Myna . . .

When she looked up, she saw that he, too, was looking at the clutter on the workbench.

"There." She pointed to the far wall. She stayed by the workbench while he maneuvered around boxes and bags and old cans of paint. He looked at the meter.

"You bring that flashlight over here?" he asked.

Jay's big yellow flashlight rose over the clutter on his workbench.

"Oh." She cleared her throat. "I'll just run up and get you one. That one, it's broken."

"No," he said. He passed his silver object over the meter. "I'm good."

Lark looked again at the claw hammer.

He turned away from the meter, started walking toward her.

"You live here long?" he asked. He pursed his lips, as though preparing to whistle. "Cute little girl."

Adrenaline flooded her body. Of course he was talking about Myna, her baby. Please be the meter reader, she silently prayed. Oh God, I was stupid to let him in.

He floated closer, baring his teeth in a frightening smile.

"Nine months!" she said. Her voice shook. "Nine months we've lived here! Where do you live?"

He stopped at the other end of Jay's workbench and propped his backside on it.

"Me, I'm Chicago," he replied.

The claw hammer lay between them, closer to her than to him, and nearly hidden in a confusion of siding nails, duct tape, screwdrivers, and last year's unused Fourth of July fireworks: a cellophaned package of Mad Dog Bottle Rockets with Report, and several boxes of Red Devil M-100 Firecrackers, Maximum Blast Super Loud.

Lark cradled Myna in her right arm and tensed her left hand.

"Marquette Park," he added.

"Oh!" she exclaimed. Her left hand trembled as though it were metal and the claw hammer a magnet. "That's where I'm from. My mom still lives there. 71st and Central Park."

She didn't add that she never visited there anymore, except to pick up her widowed mother, who didn't drive, and take her back to spend the day visiting in her own safe, suburban home.

The only familiar faces there now, in her mother's neighborhood, belonged to old people. Crime and graffiti, that was the neighborhood now. Her mother's garage had been tagged three times over the last year. Jay, what a good son-in-law, each time he'd painted over the spray of black figures, four coats of yellow paint it had taken, the message in the twisting black lines as incomprehensible to them as Egyptian hieroglyphics. Her mom wouldn't move. She wouldn't leave her church, her familiar little brick raised ranch, her few remaining widowed lady friends.

"We practically neighbors, then, your mama and me," he said. "I'm 71st and California, right by the hospital, you know?"

"Holy Cross Hospital," she said. She turned and began moving to the stairs. She could not hear him following. She reached the stairs. He was nowhere in sight.

"I was born at Holy Cross," she said loudly.

"That right?" She heard his voice before she saw him. Now he appeared from behind the wall that separated the workbench from the laundry room.

"My mother said her hospital room looked right over Marquette Park. She'd watch the swans swimming in the lagoon while she nursed me."

She felt her face burn. Oh, how could she have said that!

"They used to be swans there?" he asked. "Man, they not even fish there now."

They climbed the stairs. She could feel his body heat behind her, hear his breath.

"Marquette Park was beautiful," she said when they reached the mud room. "Well, I mean, I'm sure it still is." But she remembered the last time she and Jay had dared to walk through it. They'd stepped over broken bottles, used condoms, fast food wrappers, dog crap. And boom boxes blaring rap and Spanish music had swallowed the chirps of birds and the laughter of children.

"We have nothing like Marquette Park here," she said.

"And that why you here," he replied.

"I didn't mean . . .!"

"Naw, you not mean," he said. "I appreciate how you try." He was smiling and so she smiled back. They stood by the back door. Her muscles ached, stiff from anticipating an attack.

"Well." He blinked his awkward blinks, then chucked Myna under her chin with the silver object, the meter reader. Supposedly. Myna whimpered, but maybe it was because she was being gripped so tightly. Lark shifted Myna to her other arm.

"I'm gonna move, you know. Soon's I get my down payment. Maybe I'll go suburban, too. My kids be needing a better school. 'Course won't be nothing like this." He tilted his head toward her kitchen.

He opened the door, hesitated for one horrible heartbeat, then stepped out.

Slowly, slowly, the door swung shut.

They looked at each other through the screen door. "Maybe someday," she said, meaning someday he'd—what? Have a kitchen like hers? Her hand itched to lock the door.

He shrugged, stared through the screen at something over her head. Then he blinked and reached into a deep pocket on his pants. He pulled out the package of Mad Dog Bottle Rockets.

"My kids," he said. "They love this stuff. Didn't think you'd mind."

"No, of course not. Thanks," she said. Her face burned. What was she thanking him for?

He shook his head. "Man," he said. "I wonder. Would you be so soft with the milk man?"

"Pardon me?" she asked. "I don't understand what you mean."

"Naw," he said. "How could you? But you know, this soft bigotry I get from you all around here, it's insulting to a man." He pressed the package of Mad Dog Bottle Rockets into the screen. "Here," he said. "I'm no thief. I can buy my kids what they want."

She stared at him through the screen, her heart pounding, blood whooshing in her ears, wanting more than anything in the world to shoot her hand at the lock and click it shut.

"See," he said. "I'm taking college right now. Night classes over at the junior college by the Ford City Mall? First in my family, you know? And this sociology dude teaching the class, he say our assignment this week be to go out and violate some social norms. Write it up in a report."

He let the bottle rockets fall to the deck with a soft thud.

Then he was gone.

•

SHE CALLED THE gas company. Did they have meter readers in her neighborhood today, she wanted to know.

"Yes, they were scheduled for this week. Was there a problem?"

"A problem?" she repeated. "No, of course not. I was just wondering."

•

LATER, MYNA DOWN for a nap, Lark remembered she'd left the lights on in the basement. She went downstairs, dizzy from the chardonnay she'd sipped for lunch. Just as she pulled the cord on the ceiling light bulb over Jay's workbench, she saw that the claw hammer was gone.

No, it wasn't gone. It wasn't where it had been. Now the hammer was on top of the boxes of firecrackers. And Jay's flashlight had been tipped over. It lay on its side, turned on. And the beam was shining, like a spotlight, on the claw.

Bad Things
First published in *Downstate Story* (2010)

THE FIRST BAD thing happened when Nick was driving to work. His office was in Naperville, 30 miles from his Chicago condo, so he always left home early to beat the traffic.

He was driving his red convertible, top down. Warm June air spilled over him as he navigated quiet side streets to his office. He inserted a *Fall Out Boy* CD into the slot, looking down for just a moment.

Something screamed. Something banged his front fender.

His head jerked up. A big dog was flying away from his car.

He braked, gripped the steering wheel.

The engine hummed, crows cawed, but no voices shrieked, no horns blared.

He was alone. Unwitnessed.

Slowly, he drove on, swerving around the brown thing in the middle of the road.

He didn't want to be late for work. The dog was probably OK anyway. He hadn't been going *that* fast when it had run into him.

•

HE'D HAD A dog growing up. Frisky his mother had named it, and it preferred her. He'd come home from school or a Little League game, start telling them both his day. His mother would be sitting in her recliner by the TV, drinking from a wine bottle, petting Frisky and shushing Nick until a commercial came on.

•

WHEN HE GOT to work, he parked and inspected his car. Damn! A dent puckered the front fender and bloody gunk splotched the grill over his license plate. He fetched paper towels from his trunk and wiped the grill clean.

"What a way to start the day," he muttered as he entered his building's lobby.

Then he smiled, thinking of Tassie and their approaching date.

Tassie had the cubicle across from his. She'd been working at ANEC for only a month, and every guy in the department, married or not, was after her. She was 24, three years younger than him, curved in all the right places, a dazzling, long-haired blonde.

Yesterday, Nick had finally worked up the courage to suggest dinner and a movie after work today, and to his delight, she'd accepted.

When Nick approached his cubicle, he saw Tassie sipping coffee at her desk. He winked and waved. She blushed and waved back.

But later, just after lunch, Tassie stumbled into his cubicle.

"Nick." Her eyes were swollen and red. "I'm afraid I can't make our date tonight."

Allergies? *Shit*, Nick thought. But allergies weren't contagious. He rolled his chair toward her.

"Bummer, Tassie! I've been thinking of the Deluxe Bacon Cheeseburger Applebee's does so well. And I've got *300* for us to watch at my condo! If you've never seen it, Tass, you're in for a treat. It's an uber-chick flick, about Spartans battling the Persians. Those guys are all sweating muscles and heaving chests. C'mon Tassie. Don't break my heart!"

"Nick, my mom just called. Remember me telling you about my little brother? Leo? He's been having headaches and nausea off and on?"

"Yeah, sure," Nick lied.

"Oh God, Nick." Tears flowed. Her nose dripped. She swiped the drips with the back of her hand, and Nick decided he would avoid that hand, if it came to hand-holding comfort.

"He's only 12, Nick. We just got the MRI results. He's got a brain tumor!"

She started blubbering more than he needed to know, something about how the MRI showed a medulloblastoma wedged

Bad Things

between the cerebellum and brain stem, and he'd have to have surgery, chemo, radiation, and blah-blah-blah.

Nick's gut twisted. First dates were always the best for him. He'd been so looking forward! C'mon Tassie, he wanted to say. Shit happens. You don't let it immobilize you. His own father, working 60 hours a week at the mill because Nick hadn't been planned, had died from a brain hemorrhage when Nick was 6. Nick hadn't been planned, he'd been born seven weeks too soon, and the medical bills to keep him alive had nearly bankrupted his parents.

Shit happens.

Then Tassie went off on a more interesting tangent, and Nick perked up.

"Leo just got told last week that he'd made All-Stars! We were all thrilled! Coach said Leo would start in right field. Coach thinks this team has a shot to win State, maybe even get to Williamsport for the Little League World Series! That's been Leo's dream ever since his tee ball days. You know what Leo asked my mom when she told him about the surgery? 'How many practices will I miss, Mama? Will I be fixed up in time for the first All-Star game next month?' Oh God, Nick! Why do bad things happen to innocents?"

Nick nodded. This was one area where he could offer meaningful comfort, maybe even get Tassie to keep their date tonight.

"I know how disappointed the little guy must be feeling," he said. "Back in the day, I was the starting pitcher on my All-Star team. We were one out away from winning district. The right fielder missed an easy fly, and we lost. So I understand how bad things can happen to good people. Not to brag, but I was the best pitcher on the team. I couldn't hit spit, but man I had wicked velocity and curves. That final game, all the runs the other team scored were unearned, but I still managed to preserve a one-run lead until Lester Lispole missed that easy fly."

Nick gazed past Tassie, seeing again Lester's parents in the stands, their faces melting in dismay after their son missed the ball. They sat in the same spot every game, top row, left end.

Nick's own mother had never made it to a game.

9

"Anyway." Nick smiled at Tassie, who was staring at him, openmouthed. "I did everything right, you know? We should've won that game, but you know what? You get over it. What doesn't kill makes you stronger, you know?"

Tassie seemed frozen. Drool glistened in the corner of her open mouth. Probably she hadn't realized what a jock he was. He wasn't a muscle guy, and his oval glasses gave him a scholarly look.

"Hey! I'll bring you my All-Star trophy! Your little bro can borrow it! That'll cheer him up, inspire him to fight the good fight, you know?"

Tassie, he could see, was moved by his offer. She whimpered. He got up from his chair, intending to gather her in his arms, but she moaned softly, turned, and left.

Nick understood. Even pretty girls lost their looks when they cried. His mom had looked totally scary during her wailing jags. Tassie didn't want Nick to see her at her worst.

Nick sat, stared at the repayment schedule he'd been drafting on his computer screen. Damn. Two bad things today. Two strikes. His car dented. His date cancelled. His fingers shook as he clicked the keyboard. "Let's get it over with," he muttered. "The count is 0 and 2."

It came late afternoon, just as he was logging off for the day.

His cell phone vibrated. He saw who it was on caller ID.

"This is it," he muttered.

She didn't even say hello, howya doing.

"Nick," Camille said. "When was the last time you visited Mom?"

Nick heard the resentment in his big sister's voice. Like it was his fault Camille and her husband had moved to Florida, and Camille could no longer be her mommy's daily visitor.

"She's not exactly close by," he said. "And I do have a full-time job."

"She's in Joliet! That's only 30 miles from your full-time job, Nick."

Nick said nothing. Sweat flooded his skin. He was standing at the plate, other parents calling encouragement to him from the stands, but not with the same intensity they saved for their own sons. Some got his name wrong. Some called out the number on the back of his jersey. He was a pitcher, not a hitter. A guy great on defense.

His mom had never made it to a game.

•

"MOM'S NEIGHBOR, Mrs. VanMeter? She just called me. She went over there today?"

"Great!"

"No, Nick. Not great. She says Mom's not flushing her toilets. Her dress is filthy. Her hair is all matted and full of baking soda. She found moldy apple slices in the silverware drawer. And Mom's eyebrows are blue! Mrs. VanMeter thinks Mom used blue crayon on her eyebrows!"

"And you want me to do what?"

"Nick, something's not right with Mom. You gotta visit her, scope it out. You gotta get her to a doctor."

Nick rolled his eyes. "So, I'm supposed to find a doctor, drag her there?"

"Nick."

"She doesn't want me around anyway."

"That's a cop-out, Nick. You're her son."

"No kidding. Born seven weeks too soon. She couldn't wait to get me out. You, she hadda be induced. She wanted to hold onto you."

"Nick! That's ridiculous! Women can't control when they go into labor!"

He was choking the phone. His fingers hurt. He'd heard his mother talking to his aunt. He'd been sucking his thumb and clutching his favorite blanket somewhere dark, and he heard his mother. They'd just buried his father. He'd tossed a ball of dirt on the coffin. He could feel dirt sucking into his mouth from under his thumbnail.

"Be careful what you wish for, right?" His mother was drinking, Nick could tell. Her voice was slurred and shrill.

"When my water broke so early, the first thing I felt was relief. I could get my body back all the quicker. But he was too early. He had all those health challenges. And what do I have now? No husband! The stress killed him. It blew up his brain!"

"Think of Camille," his aunt replied. "She's a great little girl. So smart and cute."

"I don't know what I'd do without my little girl," his mom said.

"And Nick," his aunt said. "He's turning out just fine. He's a plucky little guy."

Nick listened and listened, but his mom said nothing.

•

"MAYBE," NICK SAID to Camille, "she can stay with you. Florida is great for geezers, right? And this way, your little girls could get to know her better."

"Nick."

"Camille." He disconnected the call and turned off his phone.

•

HE LEFT WORK. He stopped at a few bars. By the time he walked into his condo, it was dark. He began shedding things: keys, shoes, tie, belt, his khakis. He felt his mood lift as his stuff dropped.

He removed a mug from the freezer, perfectly frosted, and a Bud Light from the fridge.

The phone rang. His landline in the den. His mother's voice crackled from his answering machine.

"I don't feel so good, Nicky. Can you come? Camille said to call you. There's someone in the attic. I can hear them moving around. They've been stealing stuff from me."

Though he was wearing only boxers, Nick headed out to his balcony thirty stories over Lake Shore Drive. Night had made Lake Michigan invisible, and turned the cars speeding along the Drive into a flowing necklace of headlights and taillights.

He leaned on the railing and sipped his beer. He could still hear her querulous voice on his answering machine.

"Nicky! Nicky! Come on, Nicky!"

He turned and stared at the phone, visible on an end table next to his recliner, spotlit by the overhead track lighting.

He set down his beer, approached the plate, and took a few practice swings.

His mom shouted encouragement. "Nicky! Nicky! Come on, Nicky!"

He waited, swung.

Steerike!

"Damn!" He lifted his beer. "Sorry, Mama. Strike three. I'm out."

He shut the balcony's sliding glass doors, stretched out on his lounge chair, sipped his beer, and gazed at the invisible lake.

He could no longer hear her voice, just the wind singing and the traffic humming.

That was a good thing.

He sipped his beer.

Something hot and painful pulsed behind his eyes. He squeezed his eyes shut. He waited for the feeling to pass.

Barbed Wire
First published in *Morpheus Tales* (2010)

THE EDITOR WAS not talking to Missy. He was talking into his phone, quietly, in a language Missy couldn't understand.

It was her first time meeting him. She felt hopeful. Her friends who'd submitted their work had never been summoned. Their efforts had been returned, politely: *Does not meet our needs at this time. Please try again.*

Suddenly, the Editor began shouting into the phone. He shot to his feet and strode to the floor-to-ceiling window looking out over the city's downtown. The window filled the entire wall. From where Missy sat, all she could see out the window were sky and the roofs of skyscrapers. The Editor's building was the tallest in the United States, and since the collapse of the Stem Research Tower in Malaysia last month, it had become the second tallest building in the world.

Missy hoped the phone call had nothing to do with her. She'd barely done more than exchange pleasantries with the Editor when his phone rang. Now, she noticed for the first time a plaque hanging on the wall behind his desk. The plaque was nearly the size of the baby she'd birthed three weeks earlier. Black letters, as sturdy as her newborn's fingers, were burned into the wood.

The Editor Is the Barbed Wire
Between the Good and the Bad

Her breasts tingled. The message on the plaque both thrilled and frightened her.

Which category did her work fall into?

She'd pumped her milk before the meeting, and she'd put pads in her bra to absorb any leaks, but she knew from unfortunate experience that sometimes the pads couldn't handle the job. So many things could start the milk flowing: anxiety, surprise, her husband coughing blood. Jeddy's sickness after his last deployment to the space station had cost him his job. Now they needed money. The Editor had to buy Missy's work. He had to!

The Editor was no longer yelling into the phone, but he was talking fast and furious, the strange language churning from him in a musical, angry staccato.

He was not looking at her. She wondered if he'd forgotten she was even there. She wondered if it would be bad form to slip away, find the Editor's assistant, and ask for a short break to nurse. Her baby was in the nursery a few floors above the Editor's office. Her pump was in the tote bag at her feet, but the pump, she'd learned over the past few days, was not as effective as actual nursing.

It had been so inconvenient pumping these past few days. It had been an intrusive chore to keep herself in nursing status. Maybe after today she'd be able to stop.

The Editor's back was to her. His long fingers were tapping the window as he talked into the phone. Missy stood and hurried to the assistant's desk just outside the Editor's office.

Robin Rucker looked up from his computer monitor. He smiled.

"Doing fine," he said. "I just checked." He twisted the monitor so that she could see the screen. Her baby's face, scrunched in sleep, filled the screen.

"So where'd that amazing orange hair come from?"

"Jeddy, my husband—he had orange hair, too. But he got sick, his hair all fell out, and . . ." Her voice broke.

Rucker sighed. "I am sorry. Perhaps when he is well again, it will grow back." He stroked his black goatee. The goatee, soft and tight as velvet, hugged a delicately tapered chin.

"I was wondering," she said, "if I might do some nursing? The Editor seems to be involved in a long phone call."

Robin stood and floated toward her. He was tall and willowy with feminine lips and hips. He patted her shoulder. She smelled lilacs.

"I'll ask," he said, and he disappeared into the Editor's office.

A moment later, he reappeared. "Go right in," Rucker said. "Editor is ready for you now."

Missy sat back in her chair before the Editor's desk.

The Editor smiled. His teeth were bright, white, and, except for an unfortunate snaggletooth, as straight as a line of soldiers. The snaggletooth was his upper left canine, and it thrust forward as though it were anxious to break rank and slash and stab ahead of the others, like a hungry carnivore determined to take the first bite of flesh.

"I'm sorry for the interruption, Missy, and I appreciate your patience. One of our offices in the Philippines was just bombed. A suicide bomber."

"Oh!" Relief triggered a spurt of milk. The call had not been about her work after all. "I'm so sorry!" She shook her head. "I can't understand why that still happens. All the good you do, all the lives made better."

The Editor nodded. "Well, the East Asians are stubbornly resisting progress, especially the religiously fanatical ones. But enough of that. We are here to talk about your work."

Then he began to talk, not about her work, but about how rigorous his standards were, and how demanding his customers had become, and as he talked, Missy's heart thumped, her palms grew sweaty, and her breasts leaked.

Maybe he didn't want her work after all! If he didn't take it, she could submit elsewhere, but he was the best, and time was running out. In a few weeks, her work would no longer be marketable. Not legally anyway, and all the good Editors were scrupulously legal.

His phone rang again.

He frowned, sighed, lifted the phone and listened for a long time. He kept his thin eyes fixed on Missy, drilling her to the chair, so that all she could do was cross and recross her legs and smile.

"Yes," he said into the phone. "Thank you. I'll let her know. I'm looking at her now as we speak. Yes. I understand. It doesn't always work out."

He set the phone back in its cradle. "Perhaps you are hungry? It's nearly lunch time."

Missy's thumping heart settled down. Surely this was a good sign! He wouldn't invite her to lunch if he didn't like what she'd produced.

"Thanks!" she said, though she wasn't hungry. "Lunch would be great!"

The Editor pulled a pod from behind his ear and spoke into it. "Rucker, you may serve lunch now. For two."

"I hope you like crab," he said to Missy.

Missy nodded though she and Jeddy had been rigorously vegan for two years. Rucker wheeled a cart into the room. He whisked plates, napkins, cutlery, and glasses from the cart to a small round table by the window.

The Editor stood and motioned for Missy to follow. "That call just now? It's interesting news for you."

They sat at the table. Missy's legs shook.

"Is everything OK?" she asked. Her traitorous voice was shaking, too.

"I'm addicted to all things crab," the Editor replied. "Rucker makes exquisite crab cakes. We have crab flown in weekly from the Philippines. The East Asians may be shortsighted in their misunderstanding of our work, but their seafood delights are magnificent."

Missy nodded and tried to keep her eyes bright and welcoming as Rucker slid a fist-sized cake studded with lumps of white crab onto her plate. She'd become a strict vegan after her first three pregnancies had miscarried in the second trimester. And though official studies showed no link, Missy believed what others blogged on the Internet: that the buildup of antibiotics, growth hormones, and contaminants in land and sea animals could trigger miscarriage.

And it was only after both she and Jeddy became vegan that she'd had a successful, full-term birth.

Now she looked at the Editor. The table was so small their knees touched. A flake of crab clung to his chin. She sipped her water and managed to extract some crab-free diced peppers from the cake.

"Well, young lady," the Editor said as he chewed. "I must admit that I am most impressed with your work. Very high quality. Most unusual for a first effort. Better than what I've been getting from some of my regulars. They will not be happy with you."

He laughed, and Missy did too. She felt a blush heat her face.

"Thank you." Her heart began to thud again. All the careful months focused on producing the best possible, and the final bloody, scream-scorching labor of pushing out the finished product by deadline. How much money? She was too scared to guess.

"Of course, not everything is usable," he said. "It rarely is."

She froze. Her fork fell from her hand.

"But much is. Much is first rate. You'll just have to trust us now to judge what can be kept, what should be cut, what we can perhaps revise before auction."

Her breasts leaked. She knew, even without looking down, that the pads were saturated and two splotches would be darkening her blouse.

"You know, of course, Lois Silk?"

Missy nodded. Lois Silk! The famously beautiful, flaming-haired, philanthropic actress who looked younger every year.

"That call just now. She's interested."

Missy gasped.

"She's seen your work. Thinks it has the right color. The right tone. It's got potential to be the right vehicle for her."

"That's, that's amazing." Missy trembled. Jeddy, how she wanted to have Jeddy with her right now. She wanted to see the hope unpinch his face. With money, he could start treatments. He could begin the journey back to health. And they could make another baby!

"So, I'm prepared to offer you . . ." He removed a pen from his suit pocket and scribbled on his napkin. He slid the napkin across the table to her.

Missy looked at the figure. She gripped the table. Not only would this pay for Jeddy's treatment, but they would be also be able to pay for treatment for her mother, who'd been stricken with Parkinson's for six years.

"But of course, we require that you sign over all rights to this product, and give us right of first refusal for any future work you produce over the next five years."

Rucker appeared and placed a stack of paper before her.

"And. . ." The Editor rolled his pen across the table to her. "You must do so now."

"Now?" Missy bit her lip. The Editor, she saw, was gazing at the damp spots on her blouse. His lips curled down.

She began to sign. She didn't read the tiny print that darkened each page. The Editor had a sterling reputation. Rucker grabbed each page as she signed. After five minutes, she was finished. Her fingers ached.

The Editor was smiling now. He thrust a forkful of crab cake into his mouth. A bit of green chive caught on his snaggletooth.

He pushed his plate away and stood. "Come," he said. "Say goodbye."

She followed him to the elevator, which carried them swiftly down and then opened onto a long carpeted corridor. The corridor was so cold her breath smoked out. Closed doors lined the corridor, numbers on each one. Armed guards sat in folding chairs before some of the doors. They nodded at the Editor and Missy as they passed by.

The Editor stopped at door 24. The guard sitting by the door stood and unlocked it.

Missy followed the Editor inside. The guard followed her, so close she could feel his breath on her hair.

The room was small, brightly lit with recessed overhead lights. It was windowless, low-ceilinged. In the center, a wheeled cart was surrounded by a confusion of gleaming, humming machines.

They approached the cart.

A tiny form was strapped inside the cart, naked but for a diaper. Tubes dripped fluids into the arms and legs. Plastic discs attached the chest and head by thin cords to a computer. The monitor blipped a moving scroll of numbers and letters. A camera, a round black half-circle, bulged from the ceiling over the cart.

"Goodbye," Missy whispered. She hadn't seen her baby for three days while the Editor had it evaluated for genetic quality and biological health. Already it seemed bigger than she'd remembered. In a few weeks, it would be a real human being, fully protected by the laws, its rich material legally unavailable to be used by those in need. She stared at her work and saw it was good. It would improve, even save, lives, and maybe even be used by the beautiful Lois Silk.

"I expect you're relieved," the Editor said, "that you won't have to keep yourself in nursing mode. Your work is our baby now."

Missy nodded. She touched the creature's tiny nose. She stroked its wispy orange hair. She followed the Editor out of the room.

Between Hits
First published in *Hindered Souls* (2016)

I'M KNEELING IN the shed, cleaning blood off my bat in a tub of soapy water, when something crackles. I look up. My little sister is standing by the shed's window. She holds a flower exactly like the ones I planted on her grave.

"You've come a long way, Linny," I say. The cemetery is five miles from our farm.

She's brought some of the grave with her. A pulsing, crackling mass of sod, twigs, and soil trails behind her.

I put the wet bat on the floor.

"Brought you a flower, Boyd." She steps closer. The grave debris moves, too.

"Thanks, Linny. Just put it on the window ledge." I don't want her to get close. I'm uneasy about that stuff on the floor behind her.

The flower stays in her hand. She doesn't move closer. "Where's Mama? I couldn't find her in the house."

"She went to Minneapolis. She won't be back 'til tomorrow."

"Why?"

"Visiting Bruce. He's in jail there."

"Because he hit me?"

I nod. Our stepfather was behind the wheel when the car hit Linny. The other three men in the car didn't get charged. Though they were all drunk. At 10 a.m.

"I put her flower on her pillow, Boyd. Will you tell her it's from me?"

"I don't talk to her anymore, Linny. But I'll write a note telling her that."

"OK. But don't sign it Love, Linda."

"God, no. 'Course not.'"

Tears well in her eyes. The grave debris crackles louder, oozes around Linny. Towards me.

"Hey, Lin!" I exclaim. "I'm glad you're wearing the *Hello Kitty* shirt I gave you!"

She smiles. The grave debris falls silent and stops moving.

"It's my favorite," she says.

She'd worn it every day her first week of kindergarten. One week of school, that's all she'd ever have to endure. My plan was to drop out on my 16th birthday next month. By then, I'd have all three hits done, so there'd be nothing keeping me here.

I'd hidden the *Hello Kitty* shirt in her coffin, along with her favorite PJ bottoms and fuzzy slippers. She's wearing those now, too. I'd been tempted to keep the shirt; it had her scent and the chocolate milk stain. But our mom had the undertaker put Linny in the blue flower girl dress she'd worn when our mom married Bruce. So I figured Linny would need the shirt more than I would.

"There's still blood on your bat," Linny says.

I look down at the bat. She's right. It's gotten between the engraved letters of the Louisville Slugger logo. I grab the soapy rag from the tub and scrub to get the blood off. I want my bat clean between hits. When I look up, Linny is gone. So is the grave debris.

The flower is on the window ledge.

I grab the bat. Time for my next hit. One down. Two to go.

I take the flower Linny left for me and stick it behind my ear.

The Box under the Bed
First published in *Downstate Story* (2009)

DARA DUGGINS WAS still 200 sleet-filled miles from home. So, when she saw the VACANCY sign for the Lincoln Log Motel just south of Springfield, Illinois, she pulled into the lot and got a room.

The motel room was dim and musty. The rug was stained green. The curtains were patterned in the usual vomit print. The lamps on each side of the bed were bolted to the nightstands. An Abraham Lincoln with droopy eyes and severe wrinkles grimaced from a painting on the wall.

Before she unpacked her duffel bag, she did what she always did in motel rooms. She opened every dresser drawer and inspected the closet. She looked inside the toilet tank, pulled back the shower curtain, and lastly, got on her hands and knees and looked under the bed.

Most times, there was no under-the-bed. Most times, the bed was built on a platform. But sometimes, especially in the cheaper dumps, the bed had legs, and under the bed she'd find nasty things, like a dead mouse, a dirty diaper, and once, an issue of *Hustler* with profane tattoos drawn on the ladies.

She'd complain to the manager, and almost always get money off her rate. Not much, but every little bit helped. She and Leland weren't hurting financially. Yet. But he'd been asked to retire before they'd budgeted for his retirement, so she'd become more creative and assertive with moneymaking opportunities, everything from being brutally aggressive in her job collecting student loans, to using coupons at the grocery store, to staying in cheap dumps on business trips.

This bed had legs. She removed her flashlight from her duffel and beamed it under the bed. The light revealed dust bunnies and what? There, far away, too far for Dara to reach, was a box.

The box was brown, wooden, about the size of a Bible. Like an eye, a keyhole stared blankly at her from the side of the box.

She went to her car, running through the icy rain. From the trunk, she retrieved the broom she used for snow removal, returned to her room, and using the broom, pushed the box out.

She settled the box in her lap, sat cross-legged on the floor, and pulled at the lid.

It was locked. She shook the box. Something thudded around inside. Cash? Jewelry? The box had heft.

She stretched out on the bed and called her husband on her cell phone.

"*Hola*, Dara."

"Hey, Leland." She plopped her stockinged feet on top of the box.

"You not comin' home tonight? Got your favorite, homemade mac and cheese, ready to pop in the oven."

"No, Leland. It took me longer to light a fire under that loan-defaulting proctologist's butt than I'd anticipated. I'm still over 200 miles away. I got a room off Route 48. I'm about 30 miles south of Springfield."

"Bummer, *ma cherie*."

"Leel, I found a box under the bed. But I can't open it. It's locked."

"Heavy?"

"Like a Bible."

"Describe."

"Wood. Maybe cherry. And a red rose painted on the lid. There's three letters in the middle of the rose's stem, *NHL*."

"Bring it home. I'll pick that lock quick. But now, put in car."

"Why? It's freezing rain outside. And I hadda park behind the motel. All the spots in front were taken."

"Your choice, *ma petite*. But what if rightful, or wrongful, owner comes calling? Better to have it out of room, give you time, deciding how to handle."

24

The Box under the Bed

"Fine. But I think you're being paranoid."

"*Do svidaniya, ma cherie.*"

"What's that? Russian for goodbye? Or good riddance?"

He laughed.

"So, who'd you meet that was Russian?" Since Leland had retired from the sheriff's office, he'd started and abandoned many hobbies. His latest hobby was collecting common phrases in other languages. But using the Internet wasn't fair. He had to learn the phrases from a person he encountered.

"She's a cute little thing, new waitress at the coffee shop. She tops my mug without me having to ask. You won't like her at all."

"Up yours, Leland."

"*Gracias.*"

But she did go out to her car with the box. And the next morning, she was glad she did.

It was still dark when loud pounding shuddered her door.

She jumped from the bed and threw her clothes on. "What?" she shouted.

"Mrs. Duggins? This is Rulon Jeffs, the night manager. I'm sorry to disturb you. But the guest who rented your room last? He needs to retrieve something he believes he left behind."

She swallowed. Her heart squirmed. But she summoned her loan collector's voice. "I was sound asleep! Can't this wait until I check out?"

"Mrs. Duggins, I apologize, but—"

She heard a deep voice rumble in the background.

"Uh, Mrs. Duggins," the manager continued. "The gentleman says he knows right where it is. And, um, as a token of our appreciation, we won't charge you at all for the room."

Dara bit her lip. "Fine. Give me a minute." She tossed belongings in her duffel and threw open the door.

Two men filled the doorway, one short, the other tall with thin eyes and a red tie slashing a white shirt. Behind them, a cloud shrouded the moon in a sky still dark as a bruise.

"Sorry, Mrs. Duggins," the short man said. He blinked rapidly behind black-framed glasses. "I'm the manger, Rulon Jeffs, and this is Mr. Hudge, the gentleman who—"

"Excuse me." The taller man pushed past her. He strode to the bed, crouched, and stuck his head underneath.

"We'll just be a minute," Jeffs said. Sweat gleamed over his lip.

The tall man shot to his feet. He flung off the bed covers. He opened dresser drawers. He rummaged in the bathroom. He looked at the duffel she was holding.

"Where is it?" He smiled. His teeth were white and square.

"Where is what?" She smiled back.

"My property. It's not under the bed where it was left."

"Now, how would I know? Maybe you should ask whoever's been in this room before me."

"Actually," Jeffs said, cracking his knuckles. "It's just you, Mrs. Duggins. You were the next guest after Mr. Whiston."

"Whiston? I thought you said his name is Hudge."

Hudge, or Whiston, lunged for her duffle, yanked it from her grip, and dumped its contents on the bed.

She frowned, and despite the tornado whirling in her gut, she managed to keep her voice steady. "What's your problem, buddy? If you left something in this room, maybe the maid took it. Rooms are cleaned between guests. Supposedly." She glared at the manager.

"I'm sorry," Jeffs squeaked. "You'll both have to excuse me. I have some wake-up calls to make. And Mrs. Duggins, rest assured your bill will vanish. It'll be like you never stayed here." He giggled and scurried away.

"We'll check your car now," Hudge said.

"Fine, Mr. Hudge. Or is it Mr. Whiston?"

He smiled. "Mr. Whiston was, is, my associate. He stayed here before you. He left my property under the bed when he went to meet me."

"Maybe he lied."

"Maybe." He threw her things back in the duffel.

"Fine." She grabbed the duffel. "I'm parked in the back."

Together they walked around the motel to the back lot. No one was out. The rain had stopped during the night, but puddles were everywhere. By the time they reached her Ford Taurus, her moccasins were wet and her feet were cold.

"Open up."

She unlocked the car. While he searched the interior, she stared at the dense grove of pines that bordered the back lot. She shuddered. A body could easily be thrown in the trees and stay hidden for awhile.

Hudge exited her car and smiled. "Trunk."

She opened the trunk and watched as he tossed everything out: shovel, her tool bucket, three overdue library books, broom, her jug of water and bag of Snicker bars. He peeled back the rug and poked into the well holding the spare tire and jack.

He looked at her. "Hood."

She lifted the hood. He poked through the engine.

He straightened, slammed the hood. "It's not here," he said.

"I know. I don't have whatever it is you're looking for. I suggest you talk to the maid. Or your Mr. Whiston."

He nodded. "Yes. I'll have to meet with that little maid again, Mrs. Duggins. Mrs. Dara Duggins from 1610 North Pioneer, Romeoville, Illinois."

Heat slammed her face.

"So you see, I know who you are, where you live."

"Well, be sure to stop in, say hello, if you're ever passing through. My husband is a retired sheriff's deputy."

He laughed. "I eat retired deputies for breakfast, Mrs. Duggins."

She watched him walk away. After a moment, she followed, saw him fold himself into a gray Mustang, and roar out of the lot.

She threw everything back into her trunk except the broom. She got in the car, started the engine, looked around, saw no one, then thrust the broom under the car, and swept out the box. She scooped it up, threw herself into the car, and sped away.

What was in the damn box? She white-knuckled the steering wheel and entered I-55.

Four hours before she'd get home. She couldn't wait that long.

At the first rest stop, she parked far away from the other cars, retrieved her tool bucket from the trunk, and locked herself back in the car. She set the box on the passenger seat and tried to pry open the lid with her screwdriver. She looked at the hammer. It was a pretty box, but . . .

Again and again, she pounded the hammer into the lid. The wood cracked, splintered, and after a few more whacks, she was able to crack off the broken pieces of wood.

She stared at the contents. She flipped the ruined box and dumped the contents on the seat.

"What the hell," she muttered.

She pawed through the items. Something heavy filled her stomach.

She called Leland on her cell phone.

"*Nihawma,* Dara!" He sounded breathless, excited. "Where are you? I was just about to call you!"

"I'm at a rest stop off I-55, about 200 miles away."

"Do you still have that box?"

"That's why I'm calling. Yes, I've got it. It's weird. You won't believe what's been happening."

"So you heard? You heard the news?"

"No, what are you talking about?"

"Your box has a red rose on the lid? With *NHL* in the stem?"

Dara looked at the splinters of wood on the car seat. *NHL* was still visible on one long splinter.

"That's right," she said.

"I think, my love, you are about to become famous."

She swallowed. "What are you talking about?"

"*Ma jolie femme*! I think you have the box that was stolen two days ago from the Lincoln Museum in Springfield! There's an employee missing, a museum guard, a guy named Arcus Whiston. He's their person of interest. That box belonged to Nancy Hanks Lincoln, Lincoln's mother. She was a skilled seamstress and used it as her sewing box. Lincoln kept it with him all his life. On the news this morning, an expert said collectors would pay over a million dollars for that box. Of course, we'll return it to the museum. But come home fast, Dara. I want to see it first. Oh, and don't worry about what's in it. It's just some sewing stuff, not the originals of course."

Dara looked at the splinters of wood. "Oh, Leland. Have you said anything to anyone yet?"

"No. Why? What's wrong?"

Her nose filled. Tears scratched her eyes. She lifted the pieces of wood and let them fall like confetti into her lap.

"Have you learned many swear words in other languages yet?" she asked.

Silence. Then, "I've learned some," he said. "Why?"

"Oh, Leel. I have a feeling I'm going to be learning them, too."

Change of Color
First published in *Downstate Story* (2015)

HER EYES CLOSED, Rose lifted the white plastic stick from a cup filled with her first morning urine. Her hands shook.

"Please," she whispered.

Rose opened her eyes, kept her gaze on the ceiling. "Please," she whispered again. She looked down. The stick had changed. The stick's tip had changed from white to blue.

"Oh!" Something hot and fierce swept through her, and when she looked in the mirror over the sink, she was astounded at the pink color blooming in her cheeks.

Pregnant! At last!

It was 8:15 in the morning, and her husband was still sleeping his well-earned Saturday morning sleep. The firm got nearly all his waking hours.

But right now no jealousy squeezed her heart. The green-eyed monster had been slain by the blue-tipped stick.

Rose smiled at her reflection in the bathroom mirror. "Devin," she murmured. "We'll have a lot to talk about today." She splashed her face with water and wiped away the eyeliner that had smeared when she'd cried last night. She'd fallen asleep crying.

She knew it was silly to cry just because her husband was too busy at work to respond to her texts and voice messages.

She'd tried to wait up for him last night, even though he usually returned from work too tired to hear about her day or share the details of his. He wanted to make partner at his law firm.

•

MORNINGS WERE BETTER. Every morning before work, he whistled while he shaved. Every morning before work, he talked while he dressed, telling her about briefs and depositions and billable hours. Once the coffee was ready, he'd retreat behind the newspapers.

At night, back home with her, he'd shush her while they watched TV. Rose decorated cakes at a bakery. While Devin was in law school, she'd worked three jobs to pay the bills: a dental receptionist during the weekday, behind the cosmetics counter at Macy's in the evenings, and at a bakery on weekends. Once Devin started making good money after law school, she'd kept only the bakery job. She liked piping pastel flowers and cheerful messages on cakes, but now she pulled her cell phone from her robe's pocket and phoned the bakery. She told the owner she was sick. A fever. She wouldn't be in.

It wasn't exactly a lie. She studied her face in the bathroom mirror. Her normally pale complexion was infused with color, with the feverish glow of life.

New life!

She hurried to the kitchen, removed a sheet of blank paper from their printer, colored pencils from the desk, and sketched a message for Devin.

She put the sketch on the kitchen table next to his coffee mug, where he'd be sure to see it if he got up before she returned from buying the newspapers.

Once he saw the sketch, he'd be anxious for her to return. He'd want to kiss her like he used to, because he loved her, and not just because he had to jump-start himself into the business of procreation.

Rose tiptoed into their bedroom. Devin was sprawled under the covers. She pulled a sweater and jeans from her dresser.

"Devin?"

He did not respond. Well, maybe that was for the best. She was not ready to deflect the lawyer in Devin. He'd say it was too early to get happy, things happen.

But she'd already waited so long. She was not going to behave as though the outcome was uncertain. She had the right to enjoy motherhood every moment she was a mother. Even now, when their child was just a crimson speck nesting in the pale lavender lining of her womb. Her heart leaped, recalling that poetic description of a seven-day-old cluster of cells in her *Becoming Happily Pregnant* book.

Rose dressed, then left their apartment to buy the newspapers. The sky was tossing snow pellets, and the wind honed them so that they cut, sharp as broken glass, against her face.

She was glad, now, that Devin had resisted her push to buy a condo after his last raise. They had only a lease on a vintage apartment. They'd be able to flee Chicago much sooner. They'd get a house in a suburb where the morning papers could be delivered reliably and stay on the sidewalk unmolested until she retrieved them. She wouldn't have to battle the elements just to get Devin his papers. He was old-fashioned that way, wanting newspapers with his morning toast and coffee.

Surely Devin would agree that they'd want safety now, not great restaurants, a crowded lakefront, martini bars, edgy theaters. They'd want neighbors whose children would walk with their children down leafy, quiet streets, past a playground and a church to the good public school. They'd want a front porch and back yard big enough for swings and a hammock and a sandbox.

Oh, they'd have so much to talk about today!

Despite her down-filled parka, she shivered. The morning was gray, but colors spun like a kaleidoscope inside her head. Pink or blue? Devin's red hair and freckles? Maybe her large, round brown eyes? Her eyes were her best feature, though she'd endured severe myopia for twenty years until she'd had Lasik surgery last year.

Now she had perfect vision. Now she could see everything clearly.

She approached Hotel Carlos Transients Welcome. In front of the hotel stood a man with a candy-striped face. As she got closer, she realized that the candy stripes were blood. He was muttering to himself. Circles of blood speckled the sidewalk. Spaghetti strands of yellowish snot hung from his nose.

"Baby!" he called to her. He winked and smiled. His teeth were yellow and crooked and dwarfed by purple, swollen gums.

Rose walked briskly past him and bought the *Trib* and *Sun-Times* from the vendor in the subway station near the hotel.

Today they would check the classifieds, in the papers and online. They would check out the homes for sale in the suburbs. Hinsdale, where Devin grew up, or La Grange, not as uppity as Hinsdale, a healthier mix of white and blue collar families, but still good schools.

The urban pioneer life was not for children.

On her way back, she again passed the hotel. The man was gone, but his blood remained, bright red circles on the gray sidewalk. Without the man's disturbing presence, it was easier to marvel at his blood. So beautiful, like melted rubies.

She stopped and looked at it, saw how it trembled in the wind. Amazing that such beauty spilled from such damage. Had a mother ever loved him? Impossible that such a damaged creature could ever have been a beautiful baby.

But of course, he'd once been exactly that.

The blood seemed alive, trembling in the wind. It was almost as though the wind would swirl the blood into flowers and cheerful messages across the icy gray cake of sidewalk.

A man burst through the door of the hotel. He carried a bucket of water and rags. Huge vinyl gloves, yellow, thickened his hands. He crouched and began wiping the blood, smearing it, turning it ugly.

She couldn't stop herself. "It looked like melted rubies," she said. "So pretty."

He looked up, blinked bloodshot eyes bulging over purplish cheeks and a red, swollen nose.

"Yah, well. Could be some virals swimming 'round in this *pretty*, sweetheart. Don't want no one trackin' this *pretty* into my hotel, know what I'm sayin'?"

Rose hurried away without responding. "If Devin is still sleeping," she whispered to herself, "I'll wake him with a kiss."

•

DEVIN HAD OPENED his eyes as soon as he'd heard Rose leave their apartment. Now he stood in the front window looking down on the street.

He'd lost track of where she was on her basal temperature charts. He hoped this wasn't a morning she'd want him to perform. But what else could she have meant by that sketch she'd left on the table? Real cute. A pink and blue smiley face attached to a handle like a baby's rattle. Probably her not-so-subtle way to tell him that she wanted to get down to business this morning.

But after last night, he had nothing left.

He was glad that he'd prevailed against buying a condo after his last raise. It would be so much easier to make the changes he knew they had to make. *He* had to make. And it was for Rose's benefit, too. He'd tell her he respected her too much to let her be stuck with a husband who was such a scoundrel, who'd let himself fall in love with someone not anywhere near as wonderful as Rose.

"Rose," he rehearsed to the window. "You deserve someone better than me."

There she was. He watched her stride toward their building, newspapers tucked under her arm.

She was so tiny! Her smallness had once made him feel large and strong.

He recalled his paralegal's long legs spilling out from her scarlet miniskirt last night, and miraculously, he felt himself stirring to life. He touched the tender spot on his lip where Letha had bitten him, and absently scraped the scab. The wound leaked.

By the time Rose burst through their front door, he'd wiped away all traces of blood.

"Papa!" Rose shrieked. "Congratulations, Papa!" She threw the papers on the couch and rushed toward him.

Devin staggered even before she pushed into him.

"Wow!" he exclaimed. *Oh my God*, he thought.

The cold on Rose's parka stabbed through his tee shirt.

Oh god oh god oh god. She was pregnant.

"Hallelujah!" she sang. "We finally did it!"

"When did you find out?" he asked.

She stepped out of his hug. Her eyes were liquid chocolate. "Just this morning. You know, I had a feeling. I've just been feeling different the past few days. I've already calculated our due date and . . ."

On and on she went, her voice scraping his skin, a tornado whirling through his gut, she was crying now, blubbering, her nose running.

His eyes burned. His vision blurred.

"I called in sick," she said. "We have a lot to talk about."

He nodded. He had to be strong, he told himself. Children deserved parents who loved each other. And it was so early! Didn't a lot of pregnancies miscarry in the first trimester? Not that he wanted that to happen. He would do his duty by a child if it came to that. But he loved Letha. It would be dishonest to stay married to Rose. It would be disrespectful to Rose. It would be unfair to Rose. And to their child.

If it came to that.

A wave of dizziness slapped him.

"Devin!" Rose laughed. "Oh honey, you better sit down. You're pale as vanilla icing! Don't faint on me now, Papa!"

Don't call me that, Devin wanted to say. But instead he sighed and sank into the sofa. "I am feeling a little overwhelmed. My mind is spinning."

"Mine too, Devin! So many things to talk about! I love the name Lily, Lily Rose, for a girl. You should pick the boy's name! And we've got to start thinking about where we'll move. And who should we tell? How long should we wait before we tell? This day won't be long enough for all we have to talk about!"

Devin patted the sofa. "You sit, too," he said. "Take off your coat. Please." He was grateful that, despite his hammering heart, his voice sounded lawyerly and calm.

He waited until Rose settled herself next to him. He patted her knee. "First, I do love you, Rose." He felt his face blush.

She laughed. "And second, counselor?"

He closed his eyes, slipped his hand under her sweater, and pressed his palm against her belly. Of course, still soft, still flat. His heart settled back into its usual unobtrusive rhythm.

"Let's not," he said, "talk just yet."

A Chemical Equation
First published in *Passager* (2017)

AFTER THE RECITAL when he was in sixth grade, Warren started arriving a little late for his weekly piano lesson with Mrs. Muckles. He didn't want to see Simon. Simon was the student usually slotted right before Warren. After the recital, everything about Simon began to annoy Warren, from the loosey-goosey way he walked, almost tiptoeing, to his soft voice, to his blue eyes that glittered like aluminum foil under long black eyelashes.

They'd played a duet at the recital. Simon played the melody, Warren played the chords. They'd spent weeks practicing together at Mrs. Muckles' piano, an intermediate version of *The Music of the Night* from *Phantom of the Opera*. They'd nailed a standing ovation in the church basement where the recital was held. Afterwards, while everyone milled around with plates of cookies and cups of punch, Simon asked Warren if he wanted to see a movie with him that evening, then go out for pizza.

"My mom said she could drive us," Simon said.

Warren opened his mouth, ready to say, "Sure!" He was still soaring from their perfect performance. He'd never pedaled better, sustaining the chords without blurring Simon's fluid, dynamic playing of the melody. It had almost felt like he and Simon were one person. They'd matched each other's tempo and pulse. He'd never had so much fun. The music was still twitching his fingers and his heart.

Warren's father, standing next to Warren, shook his head. "Sorry. Warren's got plans." He pulled Warren aside. "Like he was asking you out on a date, that one. Keep your distance from that one, Warren."

Warren felt blood whoosh to his face. He avoided Simon the rest of that afternoon. They were 11 years old. After the recital, Warren kept his distance. It wasn't hard. They attended different schools. Warren went to the local public school in their suburb. Simon attended a Catholic school in Chicago.

For months after the recital, Mrs. Muckles kept asking Warren to learn another duet with Simon. Warren refused. Eventually she stopped asking.

•

ONE AFTERNOON, SIMON was standing on Mrs. Muckles' front porch when Warren arrived for his lesson. Warren's heart squirmed. They'd be starting their freshman year of high school next month. Warren was worried. The high school was huge—4,000 students—and famous for its winning sports teams. Warren wondered whether Simon was waiting to tell him that he, Simon, would be attending the same school. Warren kept his eyes firmly on Mrs. Muckles' front door.

"Hey Warren." Simon smiled and leaned close. "Just wanna warn you, Mrs. Muckles still didn't get her cataracts out. She can't see nothing, but today her ears are deadly." He held up his hand. "Got my knuckles tapped three times."

Warren's stomach jumped as Simon's breath heated his face. "Back off, 'tard," Warren said, loud enough for the guy sitting on the porch next door to look up from his laptop. "You're setting off my gaydar."

The guy next door smiled and looked back at his laptop. Mrs. Muckles popped up behind the glass storm door. Warren wondered if she'd heard. She was frowning. Warren decided he didn't care. It was all a sham, anyway. All these years practicing, giving up sports, for what. It was all a sham.

Simon's eyes bumped out like marbles. His nostrils quivered and his mouth flopped open. He clutched his sheet music against his gut and tiptoed down the porch steps.

Mrs. Muckles held open the door. "Hello, Warren," she said.

Warren stepped inside. Two gray cats swirled like fog around his legs. He wasn't tall, but Mrs. Muckles was so short, he felt tall next to her. Tall and grown-up and unafraid. And beer-bold. He'd drunk a beer right before his lesson, his mom clicking away on the computer in her bedroom, his dad still at work, no one but the cat to see him chug it down.

Warren strode past Mrs. Muckles to the piano in her parlor and slapped himself on the bench.

She settled herself on a folding chair next to the piano bench. A fat white cat jumped into her lap.

"What did I hear you say just now to Simon?"

"It's all a sham," Warren muttered.

"A sham," Mrs. Muckles repeated. She pursed her thin, red lips. She'd been sloppy with the lipstick. Her mouth looked like it was bleeding.

"Now why do you say that, Warren? Or are you just trying to use up your lesson time talking nonsense because you didn't practice enough this week."

Warren frowned. That was true. His plan was to keep the old witch yakking long enough, use up the lesson time so he wouldn't get his knuckles tapped with her ruler while he stumbled through the assigned piece. He shuddered. The ruler probably still had Simon viruses on it. Then again, so did the piano keys. Why hadn't he realized that, all these years? Well, he'd scrub his hands good when he got home. Then next time, if there was a next time, he'd bring a bottle of Windex and tell Mrs. Muckles his parents wanted the keys cleaned between students. He doubted any guy in high school was still taking piano lessons from old ladies. Maybe some of the girls were. But not the guys.

Warren stared into her milky blue eyes. "Can you see me? Did you get your cataracts out yet?"

Mrs. Muckles rubbed the cat's ears. "I didn't get my cataracts out yet, Warren, thank you for asking, but I've been seeing you real well since you were a little boy. And now I don't need my eyes to see you. My nose sees a boy who drank beer before his lesson. My ears see a boy who talks mean. My heart doesn't see the nice young boy who used to play so well, the nice young boy who loved music more than anything. I haven't seen that nice young boy for a while now. So tell me, Warren, what's this sham you're complaining about?"

"I don't love music more than anything!"

Mrs. Muckles pulled an envelope from the pocket of the sweater she wore over her house dress. The envelope was blue. Warren recognized his fat round cursive on the envelope. His cursive wasn't fat and round anymore. He couldn't even remember the last time he'd used cursive.

Mrs. Muckles pulled a sheet of paper from the envelope. *"Happy Birthday, Mrs. Muckles,"* she read. *"Thank you for being my piano teacher. I love music more than anything. Sincerely, Warren."*

"I was a little kid then," Warren muttered. His cheeks felt hot. "I can't believe you carry that around. That is so weird."

"It's one of the nicest birthday presents I ever got, Warren. I keep your letter in the piano bench and always put it in my pocket during your lesson."

"Well, it's not true anymore," Warren said.

"How much do you practice, Warren?"

"You know. Every effin' day."

"Is there anything else you practice every effing day, Warren? I think you still love music if you're doing it every day."

"My parents make me," Warren said. "It's all a sham."

"Why do you say that, Warren? I'm perplexed."

"Because I put out seven hours a week practicing, $30 a week for my lesson with you, $160 for a pendulum metronome that UPS just delivered yesterday, and I hate the piano, I hate you, and I hate my parents for taking $160 outta my savings account to pay for the effin' pendulum metronome you told them I had to get!"

Mrs. Muckles gazed at Warren's fingers, which rested in middle C position on the Steinway that Liberace had once played.

"Ah, the virtues of alcohol," Mrs. Muckles said. "It loosens the tongue and unbuttons the reserves of the socially diffident."

"What-effin-ever," Warren said. "I hate the piano. I'm gonna quit."

"Hate is a misplaced emotion," Mrs. Muckles said. "And your rhythm has deteriorated. Until your parents let you quit, you need to use the metronome. I've found that students like you benefit greatly when they can see the pendulum moving from the corner of their eye while they practice. Simon was just like you until he started using the pendulum metronome."

"Don't put that one and me in the same sentence," Warren said.

Mrs. Muckles said nothing. She continued rubbing the cat's ears. Warren could hear it purring. Dwindling sunlight poked through the window blinds, illuminating dust motes over the stained carpet. Warren knew to blame the stains on the cats. He'd been coming to Mrs. Muckles every Tuesday afternoon since he was 7. He'd witnessed the cats vomiting, shitting, and piddling the carpet. Warren was now 14 years old. The cats, he believed, probably numbered about 14, too.

Warren had a cat. His parents had gotten it from a litter born in Mrs. Muckles' basement. He hated effin' cats. But his parents liked the mousing abilities of the cat. Effin' mice. Warren hated them, too. Yesterday he'd stepped on a chewed-up dead one in his bare feet by his front door. He'd screamed. His dad had laughed, said he screamed like a girl, and made him scrape up the bloody mess.

"So, what's your answer, Warren?"

Mrs. Muckles had been blabbing, but Warren had no idea about what.

"My answer to what," Warren said.

Mrs. Muckles clicked her dentures and pursed her sloppy lips. "What does all this hate you're feeling have to do with it all being a sham?"

Instead of answering, Warren rippled the E minor scale across the entire keyboard, pounding and pedaling the last octave, startling the cat off Mrs. Muckles' lap. This week's piece, a *sarabande* by Arcangelo Corelli, was in E minor, and Mrs. Muckles made Warren start his daily practice sessions by doing the appropriate scales. The appropriate effin' scales, Warren cursed silently every day while he did the arpeggios, harmonics, triads, inversions, and cadence chords.

Now he zoomed through the cadence chords, pounding and pedaling and shouting, "I spend more time and money on an effin' piano than I do on my girlfriend!"

A smile deepened the wrinkles on Mrs. Muckles' feathery face. "Now, now, Warren. Your parents pay for your lessons, not you. And you're telling me that you, an unattractive, trash-talking oaf of a boy, has a girlfriend? I think not."

Warren felt blood shock his face. Mrs. Muckles had never talked mean to him before. "I'm not ugly. You can't see anyway."

Warren knew he was anything but ugly. It was bad, looking so good. The jocks at school called him pretty. The girls invited him into their basements when their parents were gone. He went, performed, but left exhausted and desperate for a shower to get rid of their smells and the feel of their nail-polished fingers. His dad liked all the girls calling. His mom complained in a bragging way to her sisters and friends.

It was Mrs. Muckles' fault he wasn't a jock. From preschool through fourth grade, he'd suffered through peewee football, Little League baseball, AYSO soccer, park district basketball. He played a lot because his father was always one of the coaches. He got stomach aches a lot, too, dreading the post-game scoldings from his father over how he didn't hustle enough, acted afraid of the ball at the plate, ducked instead of headbutting the soccer ball, never raised his hands to signal for the basketball in the paint.

And then one basketball game he'd jammed his fingers trying to steal the ball. He couldn't play piano for a while. He showed up at Mrs. Muckles with swollen fingers. "I hate playing all these sports," he'd told her. "I love music. That's all I want to do."

Mrs. Muckles called his parents.

"Your son is gifted. His fingers are precious."

And that was the end of sports, to Warren's great relief.

But not anymore. Now he resented his parents for giving in to the old lady, taking him out of sports. He could have been one of the jocks, a broken nose healing crooked, a cut over the eye, an occasional fat lip protecting him from the pretty boy curse.

Mrs. Muckles was talking. He tuned her back in. "I don't need eyes to see you, Warren. There are pimples in your voice and fat in your breath."

"Effin," Warren muttered. He was starting to feel dizzy. He swallowed a burp sour with beer.

"I can tell you something about sham, Warren," Mrs. Muckles said. "A sham is when you spend a lot of energy living a lie. E is for energy, right? It's like a chemical equation. Add 'E' to sham, you get shame. Add shame to a nice young boy, and you get mean and angry and hate."

"Uh, yeah, whatever, so, should I do my arpeggios?" Warren's stomach twisted and churned. Now he wanted the talk to stop and the lesson to start.

"A sham is a nice young man who marries and fathers but can't love true. And that was my Franco, Warren. So I know all about sham and shame and how destructive they are. And though I am forever grateful for the wonderful children and grandchildren I got from my marriage to Franco, if I could do it all over again, I wouldn't. I'd find a man who loves women. Do you understand what I'm saying, Warren?"

"You're calling me gay!" Warren gasped. "I'm telling my parents. They'll haul your ass to court. They'll sue the hell outta you!"

"Tell your parents someday," Mrs. Muckles said quietly. "Not today, but someday. But tell yourself today, Warren. Get rid of the sham. Get rid of the shame. And you'll get rid of the hate. Hate is a misplaced emotion."

Warren just stared at her. I'm dreaming, he thought. I'm not really having this crazy conversation with this crazy old lady. But one of the cats rubbed his legs, another jumped on the piano bench and began kneading his thigh, and Mrs. Muckles leaned over him. He could smell her mothballs and mouthwash. Her crooked fingers slid the clip on the metronome to 120.

"The fastest moderato," she said in time to the click-click-click. "Or the slowest allegro."

"Effin-effin-effin," Warren muttered, also in time to the metronome's clicks.

"Your choice," Mrs. Muckles said. "Now let's hear the *sarabande*."

To his amazement, he played it perfectly. Mrs. Muckles applauded, and something like gladness stabbed his heart.

•

AFTER THE LESSON, he stumbled away, out the door, down the steps, along the weed-cracked sidewalks, past old houses and newly gentrified houses, past the little park filled with toddlers and their nannies in tight pants and high-heeled sandals, and there, sitting on a bench looking at the basketball hoop that had no net, was Simon.

Warren felt himself drifting closer and closer to the bench on which Simon sat. Warren felt himself floating down to the bench made of metal. He sat. The metal bit through his jeans into his legs.

Simon looked up at him. His lashes were wet. His eyes were very blue.

"My life is a sham," Warren said.

"What?" Simon asked.

"What's she got you playing?" Warren asked.

"Crap," Simon replied. "You?"

"Yeah," Warren said. "Me too."

Simon stood. "Well, I'll see you." He began walking away.

Warren stood too. "Where you heading?"

Simon looked back over his shoulder, shrugged, kept moving.

Warren took a deep breath. "Me too," he whispered, and he hurried after Simon.

Coat Check
First published in *The Wrong Coat* (2016)

FINALLY, MADDIE SILK could sit.

That Steak Place was full. The restaurant's next scheduled seating was 60 minutes away. Maddie would have no more coats to check for a while. There'd be a reprieve from the icy wind that whipped in snow and shivers whenever Quentrell the doorman opened the thick glass door.

In a typical night, she would hang nearly half-a-million-dollars' worth of coats. Tonight, she had already taken a Berluti Quilted Leather Jacket (MSRP $9,150) from a dapper old dandelion head (her term for the puffy white afro that rich old white guys thought was in right now); a Dennis Basso Chinchilla and Suede Overcoat (MSRP $14,396) from the dandelion head's studly young companion; and several designer mink fur coats that likely topped $20K each.

Maddie began googling the furs on her phone. Damn, she was chilled. One of those furs would warm her fast. She'd never worn fur. Never would. She'd freeze before she'd wear fur. But as long as Quentrell didn't open the damn door for a while, she wouldn't freeze.

Quentrell was technically not a doorman. He supervised a team of three parking attendants. He only parked cars during the rush. The rest of the time he preferred to stand regally by the door and play doorman.

Doormen and valet parking attendants could dress for brutal Chicago winters. Maddie, stationed near the entrance, had to wear a white shirt that showed plenty of cleavage, a black pencil skirt that showed plenty of leg, and blood red heels no one could see unless they leaned over the coat check counter and watched her hang or retrieve their coats.

She was pretty sure nobody watched. To the customers, she was just part of the invisible infrastructure supporting the dining delights they deserved.

Maddie's cell phone chirped. A text from Quentrell. A joke.
Only thing doormen like bout rich fulks is their money.
Nothing from Lester.

She sighed, texted *luv u missing u* to Lester, and then texted Quentrell: *Thx for the typo!! U given me a polite way to F-Bomb the next bad tipper!*

He texted right back.
Hope u know typo was consonant not vowel.
She laughed, texted a smile, then began whispering to herself.

"Hope you fulks enjoyed your meal. Hope you fulks enjoyed your meal."

She kept repeating it until she was satisfied she'd weakened the long OH sound in folks just enough to make them wonder. Maybe they'd frown, but she'd give them her cheek-dimpling smile.

Anyway, Lester would take her side if there were any complaints.

She rolled on her stool to her tip jar. Despite management's rule that the tip jar should be at the end of the counter, she'd placed it right in the middle, so nobody—no *rich fulks*—could pretend they didn't see it.

She grabbed the tip jar and knelt before a plastic bin under the counter. The bin held her stuff: boots (L.L. Bean), tote bag (Longchamp), hat (hand knitted with her own hands in crazy expensive alpaca wool), coat (Burberry). She worked in a closet but management required her to put her stuff in a plastic bin on the floor. God forbid her coat hang next to a customer's.

She opened her tote and poured in the contents of the tip jar. Wrinkled bills spilled out. A wrapped condom. A baggie of white powder (probably baking soda). And a poker chip. A $5 chip from the Venetian in Las Vegas.

A poker chip? What was that all about?

Vegas was what, 2000 miles from Chicago?

Vegas was where Lester had promised to take her when she turned 21, but she'd turned 21 three months ago. What he'd given her instead of a Vegas vacay was a blackplum-colored Burberry London Cashmere Trench Coat which retailed for $1,396 at Nordstrom.

But he hadn't exactly bought it at Nordstrom.

She'd learned, when she'd tried to exchange it, that he'd actually gotten the coat for $299.99 (final sale, no returns, no exchanges) at Nordstrom Rack, there being a small stain on the inner lining, a nearly invisible quarter-inch rip in the right sleeve, and imperfectly aligned gold domed buttons (for a military vibe) which did not line up in two perfect vertical rows.

She dug in her bag, found the poker chip, and tossed it over the counter. It bounced against the opposite wall, then settled on the floor near a glass table holding a huge arrangement of fresh flowers.

Now she'd get some value from it—entertainment—watching whoever picked it up, whether they kept mum or crowed.

Her phone beeped. Her heart danced. But the text was only from Quentrell.

Got the tens in the jar?

Oh, right. She pulled three $10 bills from her own wallet and put them in the tip jar. Quentrell's trick to shame generosity from the next cycle of tippers.

Maddie earned $100 to $300 a night checking coats, but it was seasonal work. Warmer weather marooned her to the hostess station. More visibility, less money.

She texted back: *Thx for reminder*.

Then, so she wouldn't text Lester again, at least not until he responded to her six earlier texts, she began rolling on her stool up and down the narrow aisle between the two racks of coats. Her nose filled with the smells of the coat owners: a nose-itching blend of perfume, cigarettes, booze, marijuana, and tonight, someone's body odor. At least tonight nothing smelled of moth balls, but management still hadn't replaced the overhead fluorescent tube which flickered in headache-inducing spasms.

"Damn," she muttered. She felt a headache coming on, but she knew she couldn't blame the coat smells or flickering fluorescent.

"I'm losing you, aren't I," she whispered. She clenched her fists and kept rolling. His visits had shrunk to once a week, and not on the best night, but on a Monday or Tuesday evening. He wasn't staying over anymore. He wasn't complaining about his wife anymore. He hadn't brought Maddie flowers or wine or Chinese takeout in weeks.

Most dire of all, he wasn't returning her texts.

She grabbed her phone and texted Quentrell:

So many animals have given their skins to swaddle the diners who r now chomping the flesh of other wretched animals. My coat check room is a mausoleum. U can use this in one of your poems if u want.

He texted right back.

That make u the crypt keeper?

Maddie texted a smile back.

Was that what she was? A crypt keeper?

A hypocrite for sure.

•

THEY'D MET 10 months ago at a Lexus dealership.

Lester had walked in alone, late morning, the first customer of the day. He stopped and looked at her name plaque on the receptionist desk.

"Good morning, Maddie Silk," he said. "You are as lovely as your name."

She rolled her eyes, used to the male customers' flirtatious behavior. She never let it go anywhere. Most of them didn't intend it to go anywhere anyway.

"I am here," he said, "here to buy a Lexus for my wife's 40th birthday."

"What makes you think you'll find anything here?" was her inane response, but he laughed anyway. A laugh that crinkled his eyes and dimpled his right cheek.

He was in the manager's office, signing papers for a Lexus, when she left for lunch.

She was sitting in a window booth, waiting for salad and spaghetti, and reading the current issue of *The Week*, when a shadow darkened her table.

She looked up. Lester stood outside the window, waving and smiling.

She nodded and the next thing she knew he was standing at her booth, his silver hair salted with streaks of midnight, his eyes blue as Lake Michigan on a sunny day, and his scent fresh and woodsy, reminding her of the newly framed homes she'd helped build one summer for Habitat for Humanity.

"Hey, Mr. Larkin," she said. "So you bought a car?"

"It's Lester," he replied. "I did, and may I join you?"

She must have assented, for he slid across from her and opened a menu.

"What do you recommend, Maddie Silk?"

"I always get the iceberg wedge and spaghetti."

"Hmm," he said. "I've just spent too much money on a silver Lexus, and I think I need a hefty dose of animal protein. So?"

She shook her head. "I'm vegetarian. Have been since my freshman year in college."

He set the menu down.

"You're going to want me to leave then."

Bubbles were popping in her stomach, and her heart was beating very fast.

"And why's that?"

"Before I tell you, you have to tell me. What happened your freshman year in college that put you in the enemy camp?"

"Enemy camp? What are you, a butcher?"

He laughed. "You first. Tell me why."

"If you'd taken the Animal Ethics class I had my freshman year, you'd be vegetarian too. I lost my taste for meat after I saw how animals on factory farms suffer to satisfy human appetites."

"So." He looked at the menu. "I take it the chicken parmesan is off limits?"

"Living chickens have their beaks sliced off so they can't peck each other in their tightly packed cages."

He nodded. "That is bad." He studied the menu. "Pork chops?"

"Pigs—they're smarter than dogs, by the way—spend their shortened lives in windowless sheds without fresh air, sunlight, or outdoor access. They live in their own waste, and the high ammonia levels from their waste burn their eyes, throats, and skin."

He shook his head. "That's even worse. So I'm not even going to ask about the hamburger."

"I don't blame you. No one wants to hear how cows are castrated to improve the taste of meat, dehorned to reduce injury when they fight, have their tails amputated to reduce the spread of disease. All without anesthetics. And baby cows? Their tongues are amputated to prevent sucking problems."

He sighed. Closed the menu. "I take it you got an A in that class."

"I got As in all my classes as it happens. How do you think I landed the job as a receptionist at the Lexus dealership?"

He laughed. The waitress approached. "I'll have what she's having," he said.

Maddie felt like she'd melt into the plastic seat cushion. "Thank you." Her voice broke.

He reached across the table, placed his hand over hers. His wedding ring, a simple gold band, shot sunlight into her eyes. "I hereby promise you, Maddie Silk, to never ever again eat animal in your presence, but only if you'll forgive me."

"For what?" *What was he implying? That he wanted a future with her? They'd just met! He was married! He was gorgeous! He was probably rich!*

"For owning, along with my partners, some restaurants that serve lots of meat. Our little flagship you may have heard of. *That Steak Place.*

To her horror, she heard herself laugh. Of course she knew *That Steak Place*. Everyone did. Reservations had to be made months in advance. Celebrities, sports heroes, and political hotshots dined there.

"I like it when you laugh," he said, "even if it's at me."

She stopped laughing. "I'm not laughing at you. I'm laughing at me."

"Sorry?"

"You're like the anti-me. You're rich, old, married. And a carnivore."

"Old?"

She could see she'd actually insulted him. His cheeks flamed red.

"Sorry. Not old old. I mean, you're what? Forty? Fifty?"

He frowned. "Forty-four. And you are?"

"Young enough to be your daughter."

He looked out the window. Sighed. When he looked back at her, she was shocked to see tears welling in his eyes.

"Hey." She reached across the table, touched his clenched fists. "I'm sorry. You're being nice. And I'm being rude."

He shook his head. "No. No, you're not being rude. It's just that, you found my Achilles heel. I'm not going to ever have a daughter. Or a son. I had leukemia when I was a kid. And the cure, well, the cure killed that possibility."

For a long moment, they just looked at each other.

Their lunch stretched into the dinner hour. She found herself telling him things she'd never told anyone before. She'd never been listened to the way Lester listened to her. She told Lester how she'd always figured she'd become a lawyer like her dad, who'd died of a heart attack her freshman year in high school, leaving her alone with an indifferent mother. She told Lester how her early academic sparkle (she'd been double promoted in grade school) had dissipated in high school into a frenzy of cliques, hookups, and partying. She told Lester how law school had never happened. She'd scored too low on the LSATs (due to a perfect storm of hangover, headache, and heartache) to get any scholarship money, and by the time she graduated at age 19 from NIU, she was tired of books and out of money.

Now, she told Lester, she was 20 years old, barely getting by with a mind-numbing job as a receptionist at the Lexus dealership, and living with roaches in a dark studio on Wilson Avenue in the iffy Uptown neighborhood.

Two weeks later, she was making $100 to $300 a night as a coat check girl at *That Steak Place* and paying crazy low rent for a sunny, modern one bedroom in a high rise with a view of Lake Michigan. The apartment was owned by Lester's good friend who was more interested, Lester assured her, in having a good tenant like Maddie than in gouging a bad tenant with market rate rent.

Glynn, Lester's wife, loved the Lexus he bought for her 40th birthday. Lester loved it, too.

"It's the Lexus," he said to Maddie, "that brought you into my life."

Maddie Googled Glynn Larkin and found photos of a big-boned, sturdy woman with a jaw like Jay Leno's and large square teeth.

Glynn looked a little like Eleanor Roosevelt, Maddie thought, but with better hair.

Glynn, Maddie learned, had inherited lots of money. She'd been the only child of a Sony movie producer and a U.S. Senator's daughter.

Glynn, Maddie learned from Lester, did not want children.

"It's my one big heartbreak," Lester said to Maddie over their first Chinese takeout in her new apartment overlooking Lake Michigan. "We'd talked about alternative ways to become parents, Glynn and me. Adoption, of course. But other ways too. But Glynn kept putting it off, and now she says she's too old, too impatient, to be a mother."

Suddenly, he blushed. He stared down at his bowl of meatless fried rice. "I'm sorry," he murmured. "I shouldn't be dumping this on you."

Maddie felt her heart tremble. She stood. Took his hand. Led him to her bed.

Afterwards, spooned together under her down-filled comforter, he whispered into her ear. "Thank you, Maddie Silk. I knew you'd understand."

"You will be a father someday, Lester," she said. She pressed his palm over her heart. "A great father."

And maybe someday, she thought, *we'll be parents together.*

•

MADDIE STOPPED MID-ROLL in the middle of the coats in the coat check room.

"Oh my God," she said.

The poker chip! It was from Lester! It had to be! He'd had someone drop it in her tip jar, knowing she would show it to him the next time (hopefully tonight) they were together. She'd be complaining about the bozo who'd put it in her tip jar, and he'd say something goofy-sweet like "don't call me a bozo, Mad-girl," and she'd say, "what are you talking about?" and then it would hit her, and she'd fling her arms around him as he said, "pack your bags, we're going to Vegas, happy birthday Maddie, sorry it's late, but business blah blah blah."

Maddie shot from her stool and ran to the counter. She was about to dash out and grab the chip off the floor when a blast of cold air alerted her to incoming diners.

Maddie stayed put, readied her smile, and awaited the two couples approaching her.

A leather jacket covered a man. He was bald, pudgy, short.

A leather biker jacket covered his companion. She was young, curvy, curly-haired, tall. They held hands and were twisting their heads to talk to the couple behind them.

The second couple came into Maddie's view. Her heart sputtered. Her mouth went dry.

Lester.

Lester, holding hands with a blonde beauty.

Lester was wearing his Versace Navy Wool Double Breasted Pea coat. Maddie had been with him when he'd bought it.

The gorgeous blonde wore a blackplum-colored Burberry London Cashmere Trench Coat whose two vertical rows of large gold dome buttons (for a military vibe) were perfectly aligned.

The flawless twin of Maddie's flawed coat?

"Welcome to *That Steak Place*," Maddie said. She kept her voice pleasant and her eyes on the bald man's coat.

"Thank you, sweetheart," the bald man replied, placing his jacket on the counter.

Despite the shock waves roiling through her body, she couldn't stop her practiced eye from identifying the jacket. Cole Haan Espresso Lambskin Leather Jacket, MSRP $700.

The bald man's curvy companion slipped off her biker jacket and held it out to the man.

"This thing weighs a ton," she said as he took the jacket from her.

"That's why I'm not a leather fan," the blonde beauty said.

Lester placed his own coat on the counter. He turned to the blonde beauty.

"Lola?" he murmured. He helped Lola slip out of her coat. Maddie stared at Lola's tanned, toned, bare arms. *You'll be chilly*, she thought.

"Four coats to check?" Maddie asked. Her heart pounded, but her voice, she thought, sounded calm.

The bald man laughed. "We got an Einstein here, Les." He poked a fat finger into the four coats on the counter. *"Un, deux, trois, quatre,"* he said. "That's one-two-three-four in Swahili."

Everyone laughed but Lester and Maddie. Maddie smiled though it hurt her face. Lester smiled, but at Lola, not Maddie.

Maddie pulled four tickets from the bowl on the counter. She split them and placed one stub atop each coat.

She handed the other four stubs to Lester. He leaned close.

"Thank you," he said in a low voice. "I knew you'd understand."

She watched them move toward the hostess station.

Her heart pounding, she called out, "Enjoy your dinner. Fulks."

Only Lester turned his head toward her. He smiled, shot her a thumbs up.

"Oh my God!" Lola cried. "Look!" She plucked the chip from the floor. "Lester! Can you believe it! A $5 chip from the Venetian! Now we'll have to stay there next week! It's a sign!"

Maddie gripped the counter so she wouldn't collapse. Lola had taken everything. Her chip. Her Vegas trip. Her Lester.

She watched the hostess lead them into the restaurant. Lester, an owner, didn't need to wait for the next scheduled seating. A prime window table was always reserved for the owners.

She hung their coats. She sat on her stool. She texted Quentrell.

U realize that was Lester u just let in. With his new girlfriend Lola. Guess that's how he's breaking up w/me. This is the man I dreamed I'd marry.

Right away, Quentrell texted back.

Yup. He such a cool dude he fist bump me and say howya be Quinn. Been working for the dude five years he still don't get my name right. Anyway, girl, good riddance to that rich old guy contaminating your life. The only rich old guy a good girl like u should marry is rich old guy who at least 90. Come celebrate yr liberation w/me & Mark after work?

Good girl? Was she a good girl? Quentrell was a good guy. And *he* thought she was a good girl.

Despite her sick heart, Maddie smiled, thinking how rejuvenated she always felt after spending time with Mark and Quentrell. They were probably the most stable, loving couple she knew. Mark reminded her of her own father, dead eight years now. He had a booming laugh, like her father, and could fix anything, like her father.

She texted *maybe* back to Quentrell.

She waited for her breathing to settle, for her heart to stop palpitating. Then she rolled on her stool to where she'd hung Lola's coat.

She pulled Lola's coat into her lap and inspected it. Her hands shook as she ran them over the coat. Same size as her own coat, but perfect. No stains. No rips. Her mouth felt dry. Her legs wobbled as she stood and carried the coat to the counter. Her eyes burned as she crouched before the bin on the floor holding her things.

She closed her eyes for a long moment. She opened them. She swapped coats.

The perfect coat belonging to Lola went into Maddie's storage bin.

Maddie's flawed twin coat went on the hanger.

Wait.

Maddie unbuttoned the front pockets on the perfect coat. She found a pack of Virginia Slim menthols, Visine eye drops, a glass pipe that smelled of marijuana, and a business card for a place called High Jinques whose e-mail address included 420, slang for dope.

She transferred the items to the same front pockets on her coat, now destined to shroud the young (probably drug-addled) bones of the beautiful Lola.

She returned to the coat check counter just as a thin brown woman trudged by.

"Hey, Venita," Maddie said. "Going home early?" Venita Trapp was one of the kitchen staff who mostly sliced, diced, and scrubbed.

A hair net still webbed Venita's braided black hair.

"Jus' got a call from the sitter. She sick, stuff coming out both ends. Gotta get home to my boy so the sitter can get home to her *own* toilet."

Maddie laughed. The laugh felt good. The laugh broke the thickness that had been clogging Maddie's throat.

Maddie looked at the thin blue windbreaker Venita was wearing and shook her head. "Where's your coat, Venita? It's bad out there!"

Venita unzipped the windbreaker, revealing the knitted sweater underneath. "Jus' two blocks to the El from here. My apartment building's jus' a block from where I get off."

Maddie sighed. She reached down to her bin on the floor, grabbed Lola's coat, placed it on the counter.

"Hey. Take this one, Venita. Stay warm."

"What you gonna wear home then, Maddie?" Venita's eyes glistened as she reached for the coat.

Maddie shrugged. "There are usually one or two coats abandoned by the end of the night. Who knows why. I can borrow one of those. I'll be fine. Go on. Put it on. Let's see how it fits."

It was just a little big on Venita, but the dark purple color suited her.

"Mmm, smell good too, Maddie. What your perfume, girl? Smell like that Juicy Couture. I test sprayed it at Ulta jus' the other day. That serious money, Maddie!"

"Birthday gift, Venita," Maddie lied. "Juicy Couture perfume from my mom."

What her recently remarried mother had actually sent to Maddie from her condo in Naples, Florida, was a card containing 21 crisp dollar bills, a dollar for each year of Maddie's life.

Twenty-one dollars didn't buy much. She'd spent it in a bar with her girlfriend. Two glasses of chardonnay plus tip.

Was that why she'd let wealthy Lester into her life?

What did that make her? Venita was talking, but her voice seemed far away, background music to the feelings suddenly roaring through Maddie's body.

Her anger at Lola, Lester's new love, evaporated. Maddie had no standing to be outraged at Lola. She and Lola were both trespassers, both of them trespassing on another woman's marriage. Funny in an ironic sort of way, Maddie thought, how it took being trespassed against to recognize her own transgression. Not that she hadn't known Lester was married. But she hadn't *felt* the harm. Until now.

The harm felt sharp and venomous, a poison arrow piercing her self-esteem.

"I'll return your coat next shift, Maddie," Venita said as she headed for the door.

"No hurry," Maddie called out. "The color looks better on you than me anyway."

Maddie checked the time on her phone. Soon the current cycle of diners would be finishing up, coming for their coats. They'd be followed by incoming diners for the next scheduled seating. Maddie had maybe 10 minutes of solitude left.

It was now or never.

She took back the three $10 bills she'd planted in her tip jar. She gathered her things from the bin, put on her boots, then slowly marched the narrow aisle between the coats, running her hands along the leathers, cashmeres, furs, wools.

She stopped by Lester's coat. She put it on. Too big, of course. She knew what he'd paid for it. $1,295.

She smiled. Sell it on *craigslist*. That would cover two months' rent. And leave something for a small donation to the ASPCA. The American Society for the Prevention of Cruelty to Animals was her favorite charity, but it had been too long since she'd sent any money to them. So maybe she should just leave her sunny apartment with a view of Lake Michigan—she hadn't signed a lease, of course—and go back to the roaches. Yep. She'd do that, and then she could give a bigger donation to the ASPCA.

She checked the pockets on Lester's coat. Nothing but a ball point pen. Perfect. She used it to write a note on the ticket stub on the new empty hanger.

Thanks, Les. I know you'll understand.

She rummaged in her tote, found her apartment key. She put the key in the front pocket of Lester's—her—coat.

She strode to the thick glass door. Quentrell opened it. Raised his eyebrows at the coat she was wearing.

"Was Les behind the wheel?" she asked Quentrell. She put her right hand in the coat pocket, gripped the key. She'd never keyed a car in her life.

He looked at her a long moment, pursed his lips. He sighed. Nodded. "Red Benz. You wanna know where it at?"

"Would you tell me, Quentrell?"

"Maddie, you my friend. My *good* friend. So. If you want me to—"

She removed her hand from her pocket, left the key in the pocket.

"No." She shook her head. "There's some lines I won't cross. But you know, I like having the choice."

She held out her hand. Quentrell gripped it, shook it. "Thank you, Quentrell. My good friend. For being willing to cross for me."

He nodded. Gave her a salute. "You a good girl, Maddie."

She hugged him, promised to see him and Mark later. Then she left *That Steak Place*. For good.

Crosswords
First published in *Writing on the Walls III* (2009)

LETHA KNEW AS soon as her husband walked in the door that the poker tournament had been a disaster. When he won, he'd return with flowers and chocolates (low-fat because she was trying to lose 40 pounds) and a reservation for a weekend at a downtown hotel. But the only thing he carried now was his tackle box and fishing pole. She knew what that meant.

"How's my bride?" Wiley asked. He wrapped his arms around her and licked the tender part just under her ear. "Sorry I'm a little late. I stopped at our storage unit to get my fishing gear."

"So, no weekend at the Marriott?" she asked. She was disappointed, but not mad. How could she be mad when he still referred to her as his bride, though they'd been married 17 months? It had to be a record, she believed, not a cross word between them, not one, not ever.

"Let's go to the cabin instead," he said, and when she frowned, he added, "just for a couple of days, Sweet Potato. I'll catch you some blue gill. We could leave right now! You already got the next three days off, right?"

Letha sighed. She didn't much like her husband's rustic, mice-infested cabin on the shores of Axe Head Lake. Yes, the setting was lovely: lots of trees, no neighbors within a quarter mile, and an abundance of nature. But nature, in Letha's opinion, was best enjoyed from the comfort of a recliner in front of a roaring TV. Add a big bowl of buttered popcorn and icy Diet Coke, and Letha could happily sit back and commune with the great outdoors on Animal Planet and the Discovery Channel.

Unfortunately, there'd be no watching cable at her husband's cabin. The cabin didn't have a TV or Internet hookup. But she did have the new Devin Whiston murder mystery to start reading, and at work, she'd remembered to Xerox the crossword puzzle from the library's copy of the *New York Times*. It was folded inside her book, just waiting for her sharp pencil. So while Wiley was out catching blue gill, she could curl up with her book and puzzle.

"OK," she said. "The cabin it is."

•

WILEY WAS AS dismayed as she was to find the cabin's pantry and fridge nearly empty. The only things they found in the kitchen among the mouse droppings and dead bugs were a box of chocolate cake mix, a can of frosting, five eggs, a bottle of vegetable oil, a tin of coffee, and a plastic bag containing only the heels from a loaf of pumpernickel.

"I'll give Ervil and Vance heck, I will," Wiley said. "They cleaned us out! This'll be the last time I let 'em use our cabin for their fishing getaways. I don't care that they're my only cousins."

Letha laughed. Wiley could always make her laugh. Spending a few days with him in his cabin was a small price to keep her husband happy. Her husband! It still thrilled, saying that. It still amazed, finding love after so many years and so many pounds. And in the public library of all places!

But now, looking around the cabin's kitchen, she realized she was hungry. They'd stopped at a McDonald's for Big Macs and fries, but that had been three hours ago. Her stomach rumbled. She again opened drawers and cabinets. Plates and cups and cutlery and plenty of mouse droppings, but no food.

"I'll head to town tomorrow, stock up," Wiley said.

They went to bed, Letha so hungry she was grateful Wiley didn't suggest any calorie-burning activities.

She awoke the next morning to the smell of coffee and chocolate cake. She padded into the kitchen. Wiley was icing a cake with whipped fudge from the can of Pillsbury frosting.

"Oh, Wiley Coyote!" she exclaimed. "Why'd you make that cake? A chocolate cake is the last thing I need! You know I can't resist chocolate!"

"I'm sorry, Pudding-Pops. But I keep telling you, you don't got to lose no weight on my account. I relish every sexy pound on your bountiful bod."

Letha bit her tongue so she wouldn't correct his grammar. No one was perfect. And she herself was pounds away from perfection.

"Maybe I'll ride into town with you, Wiley. Get myself away from that cake."

He stuck his finger in the can of leftover frosting and scooped out a chunk of whipped chocolate. "Mm, that's good," he said, licking his finger clean. "Sure, Sweet Cakes. But just so's you know, I'll be taking the pickup to that auto shop in town. They're cheaper than anyplace back home, so's I was hoping to take advantage long as we're here. The tires need rotating and the radiator needs flushing and the oil needs changing, and then I was hoping to check out the fishing lures at Ben's Bait Shop, but say, you know what? I bet that little library in town will be open, and you could hang out there while the truck's being worked on and I'm at Ben's."

"Ick! No thanks, sweetheart. I spend enough of my life working at the library back home. I'll just relax here with my book and puzzle."

"Well, I'll miss your company, Sugar Cookie, but I'll be back by supper, then I'll fix you a great dinner, and you'll have me all to yourself for the rest of our vacation."

Letha bit her tongue so she wouldn't roll her eyes. Vacation! A few days in this drafty cabin wasn't exactly her idea of a vacation—they had yet to have a proper honeymoon—but no one was perfect. Anyway, she was glad she'd have time to lose weight before they went on a proper honeymoon. Wiley had brought home some cruise brochures a while back. A cruise meant a swimming suit.

"Soon's I win a big tournament," he'd promised, "we'll book a nice Caribbean cruise."

Letha's salary from the library was not enough for real vacations. Her salary covered their rent and bills and insurance premiums, though the premiums on the latest policies they'd taken out had swallowed up their dining-out budget. But Wiley was an excellent cook, and when he wasn't away on poker tournaments, he always had a four-course meal ready for her when she returned home from work. Plus, he cleared the table and washed the dishes. No one was perfect, but in some ways, Wiley was pretty darn close.

After Wiley drove away, she fried up the remaining three eggs—Wiley had used two in the cake—and spooned the leftover frosting on the heels of pumpernickel. She ate, then took her book and puzzle out to the front porch, unfolded one of the plastic web chairs stacked in the corner, and settled down.

The only sounds were the wind in the trees and the gulls crying over the lake, which shimmered in the morning sun just a few hundred feet from the cabin. It was peaceful, she had to admit, and she'd never minded being alone, not as long as she had a good murder mystery or the *New York Times* puzzle. Except, she wasn't exactly all alone right now. As the sun rose higher, the bugs got busier. Flies kept landing on her arms, a pesky wasp kept buzzing over her head, and a few big black ants were crawling around her bare toes.

Plus she was hungry. She removed her cell phone from the side pocket of her blue jeans and checked the time. Well, no wonder she was hungry! Her meager breakfast had been nearly two hours ago!

"Hunger's good," she said to the bugs. "Hunger's my friend. Hunger means I'm losing weight."

She closed the book and began working on the puzzle. Puzzles were a great distraction. But soon she got unexpectedly stuck. *Six across: ne'er losing consciousness*? Hah! She was ready to faint from hunger, she was. She couldn't concentrate on anything as challenging as the *New York Times* puzzle when she was hungry. And hunger led to the shakes, the shakes led to lightheadedness, and lightheadedness led to fainting. She hadn't fainted since her senior prom, and how mortifying that had been!

She envisioned the cake, the beautiful chocolate cake, smack in the middle of the kitchen table. One slice wouldn't hurt. Her mouth watered. Her stomach rumbled.

She hurried into the kitchen, but when she reached the doorway and saw the cake, she froze in shock. Her paperback fell from her fingers. The puzzle floated to the floor. Her legs wobbled. She gripped the door frame to keep from falling.

"Scram!" she shouted. "Scram! Scram! Scram!"

But the mice continued to attack her cake. A confetti of crumbs covered the table.

There were three of them, little gray rodents with long quivering tails. They seemed to be caught in an ecstasy of feasting. *Her* cake! How could she possibly eat it now? Shock, disgust, and hunger roiled through her body, choked her breath.

"Scram," she shouted. The room spun. The table tipped, the floor heaved, and down she fell.

•

SHE OPENED HER eyes. Her nose pressed the floor. The pine floor stretched before her. Her forehead hurt. High overhead, sunshine knifed through the blinds covering the kitchen window. Dust motes salted the beams of sunlight. Outside, gulls screamed.

She lurched to her feet, staggered to the table.

The cake was ruined. The mice no longer feasted. They lay on their sides next to the cake, asleep, their bellies bloated.

Letha stared at them. They were perhaps sleeping a little too soundly. No gentle mouse breath twitched their whiskers. Their swollen little bellies did not rise and fall with little inhales and exhales.

Letha grabbed a spatula from the kitchen drawer and prodded each one. They did not squeak or scurry or even raise their little mouse eyelids. They just continued to lay on the table, lifeless as the three fried eggs she'd had for breakfast.

•

IT WAS DARK when she finally heard Wiley return. He whistled as his feet thumped the stairs leading to the front door.

The front door squeaked open. The kitchen light clicked on and leaked into her closed eyes.

His footsteps thumped closer. The pine floor vibrated against her cheek.

"Jesus!" he said. "She devoured it! Nothing but crumbs left!"

She felt his boot poke her leg. She heard the cake platter slide around on the table. She heard him laugh.

She lay as still as she could, curled tightly on her side like a baby squashed inside its mother's womb. She'd put on one of his oversized flannel shirts before she'd arranged herself on the floor. She was confident the shirt was hiding her breathing.

She'd be in trouble if he tried to feel for a pulse. But why would he? He was a lazy bum; she could finally see that for herself. A lazy bum, and a wicked one. How could she have been so fooled? She bit her tongue to stifle a sob.

She heard the jingle as he turned on his cell phone. Then his voice. "Hey! It's me! It worked! Go book that Caribbean cruise right now, Kitten. I got $100K in life insurance coming my way!"

Letha bit her tongue to stop the scream.

"Absolutely," he said. "Get the ocean-view suite. And start shopping for some new bikinis. And remember Wiley's number one rule: less is more."

He was silent for a moment. Then he laughed. "You bet!" he said. "I'll see ya at the funeral. Wear black!"

He ended the call with a wet smacking sound. Letha heard him walking around the kitchen, whistling a familiar tune. It was the melody from *Born Free*. The first movie they'd watched together, their first date. He'd rented the DVD and brought it to her apartment. Bile burned her throat.

Suddenly he was shouting. "Oh my God! My wife! We're at my cabin, the Carpenter cabin, on the south shore of Axe Head Lake. I just come in from town, and I found her dead her on the kitchen floor! Yeah! I checked! No pulse! No! No! Oh God! No, I won't touch anything else. Hurry! Please hurry!"

He started to sob.

Enough was enough. She opened her eyes and sat up.

"Don't cry, Wiley." She smiled and tossed her hair. "I'm just fine." She hauled herself up and sashayed toward him.

He stumbled back as she approached, back, back, back. His mouth dropped open so wide she could see the gold crowns on his molars. Blood drained from his face. His eyes bulged.

And then the sheriff of Axe Head Lake County and his deputy strolled out of the bedroom. The sheriff pointed his gun at Wiley. The deputy held a set of shiny handcuffs in one hand. In his other hand, he held Letha's paperback, the puzzle sticking out.

"Would you like a piece of cake before you go, honey?" Letha asked. She opened a cabinet and brought a plate to his nose. "The sheriff sent the rest of the cake to the lab. I'm guessing cyanide. But Sheriff thinks it might be that special rodent poison everyone here has been using. Says you can only buy it on the Internet from Canada. It's so potent it's still banned in the good old USA. Blue pellets, he told me. Smells like vanilla extract. He says the mice just love it. It's like mousenip. He's thinking maybe you ground it up and added it to the cake."

The sheriff nodded. The deputy smiled. Wiley trembled.

"I saved a nice big slice for you, honey. And what do you think of the garnish?"

The sheriff smiled. The deputy laughed. He had a nice laugh, Letha thought, deep and long like rolling thunder.

Wiley stared at the slice of cake. Around it lay three dead mice. Tears spilled from his eyes.

He collapsed to his knees, bent over, and vomited.

•

LATER, THE DEPUTY and Letha sat across from each other at the kitchen table, munching barbecue potato chips from a jumbo bag the deputy had fetched from the squad car.

The sheriff had driven away with Wiley handcuffed to a hook in the back of the squad car.

"It was thoughtful of the sheriff to let you stay," Letha said.

"You looked pretty fragile and spooked, ma'am," the deputy said. "And I don't blame you one bit. That took guts, what you did."

Letha felt heat steam her eyes. She bit her tongue, but one tear leaked down her cheek. The deputy reached across the table and wiped it away with something soft and white.

"I finished that puzzle, ma'am," the deputy said. "Hope you don't mind, but it was boring sitting in there waiting for your husband."

"Oh, goodness!" Letha exclaimed as he slid the puzzle to her. "You did it in ink!"

He shrugged. A blush colored his cheeks, red as ripe tomatoes.

"And please, officer, call me Letha."

The deputy smiled. "Letha, I'm Dewey."

"Dewey? As in Dewey Decimal?"

"My mama was the town librarian, Letha, and I myself took library science at the junior college. But law work pays pretty well, and, as you know from unfortunate firsthand experience, there may not always be libraries, but there'll always be bad guys. We'll always need lawmen. Job security is important to me, Letha, because . . ."

His voice trembled and he looked down at his hands folded on the table. "Because," he whispered, "I hope someday to be blessed with a loving wife and family."

His whole face now bloomed red as a watermelon.

Letha saw that no wedding band marred Dewey's long, strong fingers.

"I'm actually a librarian, back in the city," she said.

"No! Really?" The blush had dripped to his neck, making Letha think of strawberry syrup over vanilla ice cream.

They looked at each other. He was probably close to forty, Letha thought, a good five years older than she was. And though he was far from handsome—that unibrow could be corrected, and the acne scars pocking his cheeks could be buffed—but that nose! And he had no chin to speak of. Well, no one was perfect. She herself was at least 40 pounds from perfection. But she didn't feel oversized with the deputy, with Dewey. Fragile! He'd said she'd looked fragile!

"So you finished my puzzle," she said.

"Sorry, Letha. I guess I owe you one."

"I got stuck on six across, *ne'er losing consciousness*. Let's see what you put in. Syncope? What the heck does that mean?"

"Not sincope, Letha. You pronounce it sing-ke-pee. And it's got two meanings. One meaning is the contraction of a word by omitting a sound from the middle, like in the clue, ne'er is contracted from never."

"And the other meaning?"

"Well now, that's something I find mighty interesting, given the events that transpired here today."

Letha felt goosebumps prick her arms. "What?"

"The other meaning, as I know you can now see from the clue, is a brief loss of consciousness, from low blood pressure, or fainting, or the like."

Letha stared at him. "Oh my," she whispered. "That's what happened to me! If I hadn't fainted, I would've just shooed those mice away, and . . ." She bit her tongue.

"And even though you might have thrown the cake away, it being mouse-nibbled, you wouldn't have known that the mice were poisoned. They'da gone and died somewhere hidden, and old Wiley would just try again another time."

"Oh my," she whispered.

He reached across the table and covered her trembling hands with his own.

"That saved you, Letha," Dewey said. "Syncope saved you."

Letha shivered. "Oh my," she whispered. The room spun. "I, I feel like I'm going to faint." She swayed in her chair, but Dewey shot to his feet and zoomed to her side.

"Don't worry," he said. "I'll catch you."

Damaged Goods
First published in *Hindered Souls* (2016)

WOODROW CHAMBLE'S INSOMNIA began after he retired from teaching composition to untalented and godless teenagers. Sleeping pills put him asleep, but triggered brutal headaches and dizziness the following day.

He wrote a poem about his headaches.

> *Buzzards jazz my skull,*
> *drilling flesh and bone until their bloodied beaks*
> *plunder the treasure they seek.*
> *They ravage my brain until nothing remains*
> *but pain.*

He stopped the pills—insomnia was more tolerable than headaches—submitted his poem to a journal, and at age 60 found himself not only finally published but also paid: $25 and a year's subscription to the poetry journal.

He used some of the money to buy a smallish plastic crucifix which he planted on the grave of Quayle Shanerd.

Quayle had been one of his students, a lisping stick of a boy who wrote clumsy essays about homosexuality and atheism.

Woodrow had never graded Quayle's papers higher than a *C+*, except for the last paper Quayle had written. Woodrow had liked Quayle's images of buzzards jazzing his heart and had given him an *A*.

Though Woodrow had also written on Quayle's paper: *Buzzards are nature's cleansers. They devour what is rotten. Accept true manhood, embrace the Higher Power, and the buzzards will fly away.*

A week later, just before Christmas break in Woodrow's final year of teaching, Woodrow attended Quayle's wake. The boy had hanged himself from basement rafters. Woodrow stood near the casket, silently composing a poem about how suicide was a lazy, cowardly way to cure an aberration.

A skeletal girl approached. She stared at Woodrow from dark eyes ringed with black eyeliner.

"Mr. Chambles," she lisped. A black garment, more robe than dress, covered her from neck to ankles.

"And you are?" Woodrow already knew. She resembled the unfortunate Quayle, from her beakish nose to her feathery black hair.

"My brother's twin." She pointed a finger, the nail curved like a talon and polished black. "He wanted to be a writer. Writing would've saved him. You killed his dream. With your red ink and bad grades."

"I'm sorry for your loss," Woodrow said. "But you can't blame the messenger. Your brother was damaged goods. Now he's at peace. Perhaps."

She swiveled her head on her long, thin neck. "Mr. Chambles," she lisped. "This is war." She stalked away. Woodrow retired from teaching the following spring without seeing her again.

Until December, a year after Quayle's death.

It was just before the schools would release their hooligans for Christmas break. He awoke from a fitful sleep to a sound like a door closing. He peeked through the blinds covering his bedroom window.

Snow had fallen. The street lamp illuminated a skeletal figure crossing the empty street in front of his house. A girl. She gripped a box by a handle. The box was about the size and shape of a small pet carrier.

"The twin sister," Woodrow murmured.

She wore a dark garment more robe than coat. Long feathery black hair fluttered like wings around her head. He watched until she turned a corner and disappeared from view.

"Damaged goods," he muttered. He sighed and returned to bed.

Early the next morning, when Woodrow stepped out to fetch his morning paper, he saw footsteps marring the fresh cream of snow. They trailed from his front door, down his steps, until they disappeared into the street where plows had shoveled away all traces of snow, cars, and feet.

Woodrow searched his house until he found where she'd invaded: the window over the laundry tub in his basement. The lock had been broken for years. Now the window had been pushed up. Paint flakes, wood splinters, and melting snow covered the ledge.

He shut the window and checked every room.

The only thing she'd attacked was his first floor toilet. It was filled with blood, feathers, and the journal that contained his poem.

How had she known about the poem? Maybe he'd been unwise to have the library display a copy of the journal on its Local Authors shelf.

After breakfast, he went to his attic, found his grandfather's old steel bear trap. He lugged it to the basement, arranged it on the floor in front of the laundry tub, and set the trap.

That night, he held his bottle of sleeping pills for a long time without taking any. Would she return tonight? Would she ever return? Perhaps her little invasion had satisfied her sick little spirit. He marveled that he felt no fear. After all, she was only a girl. *She'd* trespassed into *his* home. He had every right to defend himself. The law would be on his side.

He took a double dose of sleeping pills. He did not want to hear the trap's snap, or the screams of the trapped creature.

The next morning, he stumbled down the basement stairs, dizzy and wobbly from the pills. A headache raged. An odd sound grew louder as he reached the bottom of the stairs.

Roo-koo-wak-wak-roo-koo-wak-wak.

His heart quickened. He took a deep breath and stepped into his basement.

The window over the laundry tub was open. A plastic crucifix posed in a flower pot on the window's ledge.

The bear trap had not been sprung.

He squinted at the crucifix. It looked like the one he'd planted on the boy's grave.

The odd sound had stopped. The only thing he could hear was his own breathing. He scanned the room: furnace, a folded ping pong table, shelves crammed with stuff. Everything in order, unmolested.

His legs wobbled as he marched slowly toward the window. The pills had let him sleep soundly all night. Now he was paying the price with a body that felt hungover and unsteady.

Get the cross, he thought as he marched. Shut the window.

As he neared the window, he saw movement from the corner of his eye. He spun around as something hurtled from behind the furnace. It flapped around his head, screaming coocoocoo.

Startled, he lost his already precarious balance. He felt himself falling backwards. His head banged into the round steel disc between the trap's jaws. The trap clamped its jaws around his skull. Steel teeth drilled through skin and bone. Pain raged. He screamed until he could scream no more. Sweat drenched his skin.

A plump gray pigeon watched him from its perch on the rim of the laundry tub. The pain began to ease. It felt far away, there, like the horizon, unreachable. He was cold. And thirsty. He watched the pigeon. His vision turned sparkly, then black.

"Damaged goods," he heard the pigeon lisp. "Rest in peace. Perhaps."

Flush
First published in *Art Dog* (1988)

IT WOULD NOT flush.

Mary jiggled the lever. The toilet merely sighed, shook the bowl's contents, but refused to swallow them.

Mary sighed, shook her head, but refused to waste any more time in the stall. It wasn't her fault that the company didn't provide adequate plumbing.

She had to get back to her "work station" and finish keyboarding the Trustees Report. It was a tedious job of little significance and should no longer have been her responsibility—there were two other women in the department who had less seniority than she. But Annette, Mary's supervisor, liked those women. They were plumper than Annette and played with Annette on the company volleyball team and went out for drinks with the "The Gang" after work on Thursdays.

And they didn't have college degrees or husbands or two essays published in *The Christian Digest*.

Mary was just about to leave the stall when she heard the restroom door open. Heels clicked across the tile floor. Mary felt her face grow warm. She sat back down on the toilet and saw the lavender snipped-toe pumps and thick ankles of her supervisor standing on the other side of the stall door.

Mary swallowed the lump suddenly clogging her throat. Her heart palpitated and her hands became damp.

"Will you be much longer?" The heels tapped.

"I don't really feel so well." Mary sucked her lips into her mouth, feeling betrayed by her trembling voice.

"Oh. It's you, Mary. You know, just between you and I, Administrator wants supervisors to start monitoring staff's time away from work stations. Seems like you've been needing more bathroom time lately than one would expect."

Mary swallowed again and did not trust herself to speak.

"I suppose I should use upstairs ladies room?" Annette asked.

It's *the* upstairs ladies room, Mary wanted to shout. And *the* Administrator. *The, the, the! And it's between you and me, not between you and I!*

But dumping on her supervisor's grammar would not get the toilet flushed. Mary stood. She made the sign of the cross and pressed the lever. Amazingly, the toilet gurgled to life and swirled away the yellowish red liquid, brown lumps, toilet paper, and, most importantly, the used tampon that should have been deposited in the metal box on the stall's wall, just as the sign bolted to the door ordered: PLEASE DISPOSE ALL FEMININE PRODUCTS IN METAL WASTE RECEPTACLE.

But sometimes that just wasn't possible. Sometimes straining caused feminine products to shoot out. Into the untouchable nasty lumpy contents of the toilet bowl.

Mary looked at the now clean water filling the bowl. *Thank you, Lord*, she silently prayed. *I owe you one.* Maybe dropping a few extra dollars in Sunday's collection basket would suffice.

She stepped out from the stall, held the door open for Annette, then hurried to the sink. As she washed her hands, she listened, but heard nothing from the closed stall.

Mary dried her hands with a paper towel and walked as noisily as she could in her rubber-soled Hush Puppies. She opened the door wide, let it bang shut. But she did not exit. She stayed inside the restroom, motionless, only her lower left eyelid twitching.

Plunk. Plunk. Plunkle.

Mary smiled, crossed her fingers. A sweet stink tickled her nose.

Click, click, click.

Silence.

Mary made the sign of the cross.

Click, click, click, click-click-click-click.

Silence. No swoosh.

The toilet was not flushing.

Mary stepped out, easing the door into a silent close. She stood outside the door, and her smile widened when she did not hear water running in the sink. She counted to ten, settled her face into an innocent mask, and stepped back in.

Annette was leaning over the sink so that her face was practically touching the mirror. She was squeezing something on the side of her nose, but when she heard Mary enter, she jerked away from the mirror. She looked at Mary. Her lips fell apart. Two pink spots flared in her cheeks.

Mary stepped up to the stall, put her palm against the door, then turned to her supervisor. Annette's eyes were wide, unblinking. Her nostrils flared. The red in her cheeks had spread to her long neck.

"Just between you and *me*," Mary said. "It must be all that coffee I drank during *the* staff meeting this morning. Gee, is something wrong?"

Annette opened her mouth. "Well," she began, but Mary stepped into the stall.

"Oh!" Mary exclaimed. "Oh, dear." She stepped back out, smiled at her supervisor. "Well, I guess I better use *the* upstairs ladies room."

Without waiting for Annette's response, Mary hurried from the restroom, biting her tongue to keep from laughing.

Oh my, she thought, patting her hot cheeks. *Bet I'm redder than Annette.*

The phrase, "flushed with success" shot through her thoughts like a breaking billiard ball. By the time she reached her work station, the opening lines of a new essay for *The Christian Digest* were itching for freedom. She put aside the Trustees Report and began to type.

A Gift from Santa
First published in *Woman's World* (2011)

FINALLY IT WAS Willy's turn to sit on Santa's lap.

Ed frowned as his grandson whispered in Santa's ear. Willy had refused to tell Ed what he wanted from Santa, but Ed had promised his daughter, Willy's mother, that he'd find out.

"Willy's being very mysterious this year," Hazel had said to Ed during breakfast. "I hope he's not wanting something impossible from Santa, like a trip to Disney World."

Now Santa was shaking his head and whispering back to Willy.

Ed sighed. So it *was* something impossible Willy wanted. Since his wife's death last year, Ed's greatest joy had been buying things for his only grandchild. If he could, he would have paid for Disney World for Hazel and Willy, but most of his retirement income went to expenses for the house they shared. Anything extra he spent on Willy.

The woman whose child was next in line grumbled, "That boy's two minutes with Santa ended three minutes ago."

Ed clenched his fists. Willy was only 5. In a few years, Willy would no longer believe that Santa could grant him his heart's desire. Let him enjoy a few extra minutes in Santa's lap, Ed wanted to scold the woman. He felt tears sting his eyes. His late wife, he was sure, would not have hesitated to say something to the impatient woman.

Willy was pointing at him. Santa was looking at Ed. Santa's eyes under his long dark eyelashes were very blue, and they did seem to twinkle, though Ed decided that was probably just from the overhead lights.

"Big smile for Santa now," the photographer-elf said.

A Gift from Santa

The bulb flashed, Willy hopped off, and the next child scrambled up.

"What did you ask Santa for?" Ed said.

Will bit his lower lip. "I can't tell you."

Santa was now listening to the little girl on his lap who was conveniently letting the world know that she wanted a white kitten.

"I need to talk to the elf about buying the photo," Ed said to Willy.

Ed approached the photographer and whispered, "What did my grandson say to Santa? Is there any way you can find out?"

The photographer winked, crouched next to Santa, and whispered in Santa's ear.

Again Santa gazed at Ed, then whispered back to the photographer for what seemed to Ed like a long time.

The photographer returned to Ed and murmured, "Meet Santa by the fountain next to the food court after his shift ends at four. Santa must tell you in person what your grandson wants."

Now Ed was worried. Did Willy want something terrible? But he nodded and waved goodbye.

Back home, Ed found Hazel bent over the kitchen table, piping buttercream flowers on a customer's cake.

Willy was fast asleep in Ed's arms.

"Did you find out?" Hazel asked.

"Not yet," Ed replied. "But after I tuck Willy into bed, I'm heading back to the mall to meet with Santa."

At the mall's fountain, Ed waited. A slim woman approached. Short white curls covered her head. Long black lashes fluttered over very blue eyes.

"I have a message for you from Santa," she said.

"Yes?" Ed's stomach hurt the way it sometimes did when he was nervous. She had a nice voice, soft like his late wife's.

"Don't take this wrong," the woman said.

"Uh oh," Ed muttered.

"Your grandson has the right stuff," she said. "All he wants is what he thinks *you* need to be happy."

"I am happy!"

She shrugged. He caught a whiff of her perfume, the scent of cinnamon and apples.

"He told me his grandma died last year. He told me you hardly smile anymore."

"So he wants me to smile more? I can do that!" And to prove it, Ed forced his lips into a big smile. "Happy?"

"Well, there is one more thing."

"What?"

"Again, don't take this the wrong way."

"What!"

"Your grandson thinks a new grandma would make you happy."

"What?"

Her blue eyes never left his face.

Ed sighed. "I didn't realize he'd picked up on my feelings like that. Tell Santa I thank him for letting me know."

"You're welcome," she replied.

Her blue eyes twinkled under long dark lashes. It clicked. "*You're* Santa?" Ed exclaimed.

She nodded. "This Santa gig has been in my life a long time. My husband was Santa at this mall for years until he passed away. I took over. Best job I've ever had."

"Are they looking for subs?" Ed heard himself say.

"Are you interested?" she replied.

"Do you have time to talk about it over coffee?" he asked.

She held out her hand. "My name's Meredith. But friends call me Merry."

"Merry," Ed repeated. He clasped her hand and smiled.

Handshake of Peace
First published in *St. Anthony Messenger* (2013)

THE GROCERY STORY across the street from St. Joe's was crowded with post-Mass shoppers. Lucy hadn't eaten breakfast. She felt empty. Everything looked good. She stopped by the meats and scowled at the rib roasts.

Buy One Get One Free proclaimed the sign.

"I don't need two roasts," she muttered.

She hadn't meant to be heard, but another shopper looked at her a little too long. His eyes narrowed as though he were seeing something offensive. She recognized him from church. He'd been seated across the aisle from her next to a pretty blonde woman. During the handshake of peace, she'd seen them hug each other.

"Those the real deal?" he asked. His right hand rested on the handle of his shopping cart. His left hand was in the pocket of his blue jeans.

He pointed at the dog tags around her neck, his finger so close she backed away. Short brown hair hugged his scalp. A scar etched a crescent under his left eye.

Mind your own business, Lucy thought. But he was wearing a Chicago White Sox tee shirt (her father had loved that team), and a gold cross on a chain around his neck, so she answered his question.

"My dad's. Vietnam."

"That's good. I mean, then you have a right to wear them."

She frowned. *Who are you,* she thought, *the dog tag police?*

"Sorry." He rubbed the scar under his eye. "I can see I've offended you. It's just that you see rappers wearing dog tags now. Teenagers. Celebrities. They don't have the right."

She stared at him. Her on-again off-again boyfriend, the front man for a local rock group, wore dog tags when he performed at clubs—authentic tags he'd bought on *craigslist*.

"I'll let you get on with your shopping," he said. He grabbed his cart and moved off.

She felt her posture droop as she watched him walk away. He moved fluidly, with perfect posture. *I'm here for groceries,* she told herself, *not to hook up with a potential stalker. Even if he is cute.*

Not my type anyway, she decided. *A dog tag junkie whose only soldiering happens in video games.*

Not like her father.

Lucy fingered the dog tags while she considered the roasts. Maybe two smallish ones. No. There was no room in her freezer for the extra roast. Her freezer was crammed with boxes of single-serve frozen meals. Since her father's death from leukemia last year, grocery shopping had gotten a lot simpler. And lonelier.

"I don't want to buy two roasts either."

Lucy looked up. The man was back. His cart held only a quart of milk. His blue eyes were the color of his faded jeans.

"Why can't the store just offer one at half price?" he asked.

Lucy nodded. "Did you see the Russet potatoes? Today's it's buy one 10-pound bag, get the other free. Maybe I could use up the first bag before they went soft, but the second? No way."

Stop babbling, she silently scolded herself. *Twenty-six is too old to get flustered when a good-looking guy pays attention to me.*

"Those the original silencers?" He was looking at her dog tags again.

"Excuse me?"

"The black rubber around your dog tags. Vietnam was when American soldiers were allowed to place rubber silencers on their tags so the enemy couldn't hear the metallic clanking."

"I know what silencers are. I'm just wondering why you're grilling me about these tags. I mean, you're wearing a White Sox tee, but it's not my business whether you're a true fan. And you're wearing a cross, but it's not my business whether you go to church every Sunday."

He blushed. "You're right. But for the record, I am a Sox fan, and I do go to church. As a matter of fact, I saw you at the 10 o'clock Mass."

"I saw you, too," she said. "With a pretty blonde."

"That wasn't a pretty blonde. That was my sister."

Lucy laughed. "So sisters can't be pretty blondes?"

"Not from a brother's point of view, I guess."

"And to that," Lucy replied, "I can only say, oh brother."

"I'm staying with my sister until I find a place I can afford on a new teacher's salary." He waited a beat, but Lucy said nothing. She knew she was supposed to ask him where he was teaching, but there was something unsettling about him, despite his good looks. There was something serious in his face, intense in his eyes. Her father had had the same intensity, eyes that had seen too much, eyes that could suddenly explode into rage or glaze from drink. Eyes that drilled, a mouth that flatlined.

"You go to St. Joe's?" he asked.

She nodded, felt her own face heat at the tiny lie. She rarely attended Mass anymore. She *used* to go. With her father every Sunday from the time she was little until she'd left for college. The 10 o'clock Mass. Third pew from the altar. Afterwards, she'd stand next to her dad while he lit two candles in the back of the church. "For my brothers," he'd murmur as he lit the first candle. He'd remove a $5 bill from his wallet and drop it into the box. "For your mom and baby sister," he'd say to Lucy as he lit a second candle. He'd give Lucy another $5 and she'd push it through the payment slot.

His brothers were the soldiers on his team who'd defoliated the perimeters of military bases in Vietnam with Agent Orange, an herbicide containing dioxin.

The $10 he paid for the candles every Sunday came from what he called his 'Orange money.' Ten years after the war ended, he received $180,000 as part of a class action settlement from the chemical companies who'd manufactured and sold Agent Orange during the Vietnam War. It turned out they'd done so with full knowledge of the serious health risks.

Lucy blamed her dad's chronic leukemia and alcoholism on Agent Orange. And all the miscarriages her parents had endured until finally she'd been born. And the two deaths in a car accident when Lucy was 10. Her mom behind the wheel, driving Lucy's baby sister somewhere. The baby severely disabled with spina bifida.

Broad daylight. Good weather. But her mother had crashed into a tree.

Leukemia. Miscarriages. Spina bifida. Her mother's depression over the miscarriages and the final baby, born wrong.

Lucy blamed Agent Orange. And the war. She vowed she'd never get involved with a soldier.

•

"THEY HAVE GOOD sermons at St. Joe's?"

He was smiling at her. The smile transformed his face. He wasn't just cute, Lucy realized. He was really cute.

"The *music* is beautiful," she said.

His mouth wasn't smiling anymore, but his eyes were. Lucy felt certain that he was a man who didn't smile much.

"So I'm guessing you *don't* like the sermons," he said. He moved back to let a woman with a nearly full shopping cart get easier access to the rib roasts. Lucy watched the woman briskly select a pair of roasts and move off.

"She probably has a big freezer in her basement," Lucy said. "Guess that's something I'll have to get if I ever hope to take advantage of these buy one get one free deals."

"Hey," the man said. Another smile transformed his face. "How about we team up right now? One of us pays at checkout for the double items, then we divvy up afterwards."

Lucy moved the dog tags back and forth on the chain around her neck. "I don't know," she said.

She looked at his hands to make sure there was no wedding ring or telltale pale skin where a ring would be.

Only his right hand rested on the cart handle. His left hand was in the pocket of jeans.

"I'm not married," he said. "Never have been."

"Then why are you hiding your left hand?"

He sighed. Removed his left hand from his pocket, placed it on the handle of the cart.

She blinked. "Oh!" she gasped, then she coughed to disguise her reaction.

His left hand was wrong. Its skin was rough and mottled. And most shocking, there was nothing between his thumb and fifth finger. Just squat stubs of scarred flesh over the knuckles.

"War injury," he said. He lifted his damaged hand. "Sorry if it scares you."

"It doesn't scare me," she said. But it did. A damaged soldier. Like her father. She'd suffered the damage war had done to her father, the collateral damage to her mother.

"Happened in Afghanistan," he was saying. "I was in the National Guard, walking back to base from patrol. A little girl ran up to us. Held up a bowl of dried apricots. 'For you, for you,' she said. She had such a sweet smile. She was wearing this huge *Hello Kitty* tee shirt and long skirt. She couldn't have been more than 10 years old. I grabbed a handful of apricots, walked on. I turned around, lifted my left hand to wave goodbye. A bunch of the guys were around her. She blew up."

Lucy felt dizzy. Why was he telling her this awful story? They were strangers. She didn't even know his name.

"I'm sorry," she murmured.

He shrugged. "Turns out there was an improvised explosive device strapped to her waist under the tee shirt. Some guys were killed. My buddy lost his eyes. I guess I was lucky. The only damage is my scar and my hand."

Only visible damage, Lucy thought. She looked at her wrist watch. "Oh! I've got to get going. I've got people coming for dinner." She felt the lie warm her cheeks.

"It was nice meeting you." He extended his undamaged right hand. "I'm Leo."

"Lucy." She quickly shook his hand. "Nice meeting you."

"Too much information, I guess." He sighed. "I'm sorry I dropped all that on you. I guess I figured your dad being a vet . . ."

She shook her head, began pushing her cart away. "It's OK, really," she said over her shoulder as she moved up the aisle. "I really do have to get going." Her heart pounded. When she got to the checkout lanes, she pushed her cart with its few items off to the side and left the store.

As she drove home, she reassured herself: *Dodged that bullet.*

But all week she thought about Leo. She saw his ruined hand while she listened to her students perform their scales on her piano. She recalled his clear blue eyes while she decorated cakes at the bakery. Her heart quickened when she remembered how the two smiles he'd offered her had transformed his face. She wondered where he was teaching. A new teacher, he'd said. Her father, too, had been a teacher. High school U.S. History for 20 years until his chronic leukemia had sidelined him, then killed him.

On Thursday, when her sometime-boyfriend texted her suggesting that she come to the club where his band had a gig, she deleted the message without replying.

On Saturday evening, she joined her girlfriends for a movie, but then begged off going for drinks afterwards. She knew a late night would make it harder to get up before noon on Sunday.

•

ON SUNDAY MORNING, she found herself pulling into St. Joe's parking lot for the 10 o'clock Mass. She was early. The parking lot was half empty.

Inside the church, she stood in the back, scanning the pews. She saw Leo in the same pew he'd been last week. Her stomach jumped. There was no pretty blonde sister sitting next to him.

She went to the rack of candles and lit one. "For all the soldiers," she whispered.

She removed a $20 bill from her purse, dropped it into the payment slot.

She lit another candle.

"For those who love the soldiers," she murmured. She clasped the dog tags around her neck. "And for those who will love them."

She walked up the aisle, slipped into the pew behind Leo.

During the handshake of peace, when he turned around and saw her, his eyes widened. He didn't return her smile.

She extended both her hands. He hesitated, just a moment, then placed both his hands in hers. His hands felt warm. His expression was cold.

"Peace be with you," she said.

He lifted his eyes from their hands to her face. At last he replied, "And with you too."

"Grocery shopping after church?" Her heart was beating so fast. His hands still filled hers.

He nodded. "You?"

She nodded, too.

And then, at last, he smiled.

Innuendoes
First published in *St. Anthony Messenger* (2012)

MISS GRIMM PAID Evita Navarro a dollar a day to walk Lady once in the morning before school, once in the afternoon after school. Evi lived with her mother and little brother Freddy in the apartment building next to Miss Grimm's house. This was Evi's first job, and though in the beginning she wanted to like her boss, she found that she couldn't. Evi would've hated Miss Grimm if hating hadn't been a sin. But she no longer felt guilty about disliking the old woman, not since Evi's mother had explained that most people didn't much like their bosses. It was just how it was.

"Neighborhood's too dangerous for someone like me now," Miss Grimm had said to Evi during the job interview. "Even accompanied by a big strong dog like Lady."

Evi felt her cheeks grow hot, and if Lady hadn't been watching Evi with such beautiful brown eyes, Evi might have declined the job, despite her need for money to pay for a cell phone. Everyone in Evi's sixth grade class had cell phones. Everyone but Evi.

"Why doesn't she move if she thinks the neighborhood is so dangerous?" Evi asked her mother later.

"The neighborhood is not so dangerous," her mother replied. "That old woman is just making an innuendo. Dangerous is her code for the neighborhood being more Hispanic these days than the German and Irish it used to be."

"Innuendo," Evi repeated. She liked how the word felt bouncy and musical, like her father's Spanish words when he sang.

Her mother hated when he sang. He sang only when he drank. But Evi liked her father best when he sang.

Evi's mother had been born in Puerto Rico, but had lived in Chicago since she was 2. Evi's father had come from Mexico, illegally. He'd washed dishes at the club where Evi's mother hostessed and modeled. They'd never legally married. Evi's father thought it too risky to appear before any officials. So when Freddy, Evi's little brother got sick, it was easy for her father to leave.

•

OUTSIDE MISS GRIMM'S back door, Evi removed a towel from a box and wiped Lady's paws. They entered Miss Grimm's dark kitchen. It smelled of cigarettes and the blue cheese Miss Grimm squeezed into her martini olives.

Miss Grimm sat at the table, sipping a martini. Stuff cluttered the table: a large print edition of *Reader's Digest*, a bowl filled with rosaries, a plate of anchovies, a two-foot high statue of St. Jude, his nose chipped, his sandaled feet on the verge of stepping into a full ashtray.

"She do all her business?" Miss Grimm asked.

Evi nodded and unhooked the leash from Lady's collar. Lady stretched herself over Evi's feet.

"How's my baby?" Miss Grimm leaned forward and rubbed Lady's cropped boxer ears. "How's my good girl?" Miss Grimm sat back, groaned, rubbed her back.

"Oh, my aching bagel." She squinted at Evi, waved her hand under her nose as though Evi had brought in a bad smell.

She did that every afternoon while Evi waited for the crumpled dollar bill Miss Grimm plucked from the pocket of the flower-patterned house dress she always wore.

The first time Evi had worried that she'd brought a bad smell into the house. But her mother explained. "She's trying to make you think you smell bad, honey. It's another innuendo. But what's smelling bad, Evi, is that old lady's manners, not you."

•

"YOU KEEP HER on-leash?" Miss Grimm asked.

Evi nodded, her fingers crossed behind her back so she wouldn't have to add this lie to her confession list. Lady liked to chase squirrels, so Evi always unleashed Lady as soon as they crossed the busy street.

"How's your father?"

"He's fine." Evi crossed her fingers tighter. She'd seen Miss Grimm peering out the window three months earlier, watching Evi's father load all his belongings into the back of a pickup truck and drive away.

"My parents raised five kids on a baker's wages. Never needed food stamps or Section Eight housing like that apartment building you're in."

Lady grunted and pushed her wet nose into Evi's hand. Evi's heart beat fast. Her cheeks felt hot.

"I pray for your family every day." Miss Grimm pointed to the St. Jude statue. "Patron saint of lost causes."

Another innuendo, Evi thought. "Thank you," she murmured.

At last, Miss Grimm placed a dollar on the table.

•

LADY STRAINED AT the leash as they waited to cross the busy street. Traffic was worse since the new county hospital had opened a mile east. Lady pulled and pulled, pulled Evi off the curb into the street. A speeding car honked and swerved, just missing them.

"Lady! Bad girl!" Evi yanked the boxer back to the curb. And before she could stop herself, she punched Lady's back, hard, three times.

Lady whimpered. Evi fell to her knees, hugged the dog. "I'm sorry, girl." A memory put goosebumps on her arms: her father hugging her mother after his slaps, kissing her mother's tears.

Lady licked Evi's face. Evi bit her tongue. The pain made her father and other confusing memories go away.

Hitting Lady, she knew, was another sin to add to her confession list.

"I'll make it up to you, Lady," Evi whispered.

As soon as they turned into the alley, Evi removed Lady's leash. Lady squatted next to Evi, looked up at her. "Go girl," Evi said. "Go. Have fun."

Lady leaped away, bouncing after birds and drifting litter, and then, barking, she charged a squirrel.

Evi's stomach hurt. She shouldn't have hit Lady. Maybe her father, when he'd slapped her mother, maybe he'd felt bad too.

So why did people hit those they loved?

"I won't ever hit again," Evi whispered. "I promise you, God."

The squirrel shot down the alley, Lady in close pursuit, and when the squirrel neared the busy street, Evi screamed. "Lady! Heel!"

But Lady raced after the squirrel.

Into the busy street.

A red convertible screeched and slammed to a stop. Horns blared, cars swerved around the convertible.

Evi ran, the useless leash slapping against her legs as she ran, ran, ran.

By the time she reached Lady, the driver had parked his convertible at the curb and carried Lady off the street. He laid her on the grassy parkway.

"I'm so sorry," the driver said. He crouched next to Lady.

Evi could see that Lady was gone, her beautiful head crushed, blood, bones, and brain where once had been sparkling brown eyes and velvet nose and alert ears, always flicking at sounds.

Evi collapsed to her knees. "Oh, Lady, Lady, Lady," she moaned.

"I hit your dog, miss. She came out of nowhere. I couldn't stop. Another car rolled over her. It just kept going. But it was my fault. I'm the one who hit her first."

The driver stood. Evi looked up at him. He was short, soft-looking, with a round belly and bubbly brown hair fringing a bald head. Blood splotched his white shirt.

He handed her a card. "Give this to your parents. They can call me, and I'll be happy to pay for a new dog. But I have to go now. I've got a patient in labor. That's where I was heading. The hospital."

But as he moved to his car, Miss Grimm came flying from her house, shrieking, her long gray hair and flower-patterned house dress billowing behind her.

"My baby! My baby!" she screamed. She yanked Evi's hair. "What did you do? The leash! Why isn't my Lady on-leash?"

The driver placed his hand on Miss Grimm's shoulder. "Ma'am, it's my fault."

She released Evi's hair and faced him.

"I'm Dr. Abraham. I hit your granddaughter's dog. It's my fault. I'll pay for a new dog for you."

"Granddaughter? She look like she could be my granddaughter? I paid this girl good money to walk my dog. And I told her to always, always keep Lady on her leash."

Miss Grimm yanked Evi's hair again. "Didn't I? And didn't you always tell me you were keeping her on-leash? Look what happened!"

Evi could hardly see through her tears. She stroked Lady's still-warm body. The fur was sticky with blood.

"I'm so sorry," Evi sobbed.

"Ma'am, what's your name?" Dr. Abraham pulled a check book and pen from an inside pocket of his suit jacket. "I'll write a check right now."

Miss Grimm squinted at him. "Grimm," she said. "G-R-I-M-M. Agnes. Grimm."

"Suits you," he murmured.

"What?"

"What do you need to buy another dog?"

Miss Grimm clicked her teeth. "Five thousand dollars. Shots, dog tags, gotta pay for all that again, plus taxi fare to take a new dog to vet appointments. I don't drive anymore. Not safe, not with all these uninsured illegals behind the wheel these days. All these pork chops, tacos, beanos, ruining what used to be a perfectly good neighborhood."

Dr. Abraham shook his head and began writing a check. "I'll pay you $500," he said.

He tore off the check, held it out. After a moment, Miss Grimm grabbed it, studied it, then pushed it into the pocket of her house dress.

"You know," he said. "I actually like pork chops, tacos, and beans. In fact, the only thing I absolutely despise is sauerkraut."

Despite her sorrow, Evi smiled. An innuendo. Dr. Abraham had made an innuendo.

Innuendoes

"Well, doctor," Miss Grimm said. "You best be taking care of my Lady's body, too. This *sour kraut* is too old to be digging a grave."

Miss Grimm's shoulders sagged. Evi watched her shuffle away. She could hear her crying, and suddenly, for the first time, Evi felt sorry for the old woman.

"It's my fault," Evi said.

"What's your name?" Dr. Abraham asked.

"Evita. Evi."

"Evi, I'll take Lady with me. Don't worry about it. It wasn't your fault."

"No! Please! Do you think, maybe, you could bring her to my yard? I could bury her under the crab apple tree."

Dr. Abraham sighed. He looked at his watch.

He lifted Lady, cradled her against his chest. He followed Evi to the square of weedy grass behind her apartment building.

"I'll come back after I deliver my patient's baby," he promised. "I'll dig the grave. Tomorrow. OK, Evi?"

That evening, Evi and her mother knelt before Lady's body under the tree. They tugged a large black trash bag over the dog. Evi tied the bag with red ribbon. Walking back to the apartment building, Evi glanced up. Miss Grimm stood in her kitchen window, staring at her.

The next morning, when Evi peered out her bedroom window into the yard, Lady's body still formed a lump under the tree. But now it was covered with a flowered house dress.

●

DR. ABRAHAM ARRIVED late in the afternoon. He carried two shovels. He kept looking at Evi's mother.

"Tell your husband I'm sorry for all this trouble I've caused," he said.

"There's no husband to tell," she replied.

Color flooded his cheeks.

"I'm Jay. Jay Abraham."

"Maria Navarro," Evi's mother replied.

●

EVI AND HER mother helped Dr. Abraham dig the grave. Evi's brother Freddy watched from his wheelchair. Evi kept glancing at Miss Grimm's house, but the windows remained empty. She grabbed the dress covering Lady and flung it off.

Dr. Abraham pulled the trash bag containing Lady's body to the edge of the grave. Together, they knelt and pushed the dog into the grave.

"What about the dress?" he asked.

"It's Miss Grimm's," Evi said.

"Yuck," Freddy said. He rolled his wheelchair away from the dress. "Throw it away."

Evi looked at Miss Grimm's house. The old lady was standing behind her kitchen window, looking at them.

Evi lifted the dress. She stood over the grave, released it, and watched it float down over Lady. She looked back at the window. Miss Grimm was gone.

•

IT DIDN'T TAKE long for them to fill the grave.

"Could I take the three of you to dinner sometime?" Dr. Abraham asked. "I'll bet you know all the good Mexican restaurants around here."

His face reddened. "What I mean is, I love Mexican food."

Evi's mother smiled. "I'm Puerto Rican. But I love Mexican food, too. Sure. Sometime would be great."

"How about now?" he asked.

"Yeah, Mama, I'm starving!" Freddy shouted. Evi rolled her eyes at her little brother.

"OK," Evi's mother said. "Just give us a bit of time to make ourselves presentable."

Evi skipped to her bedroom. As she searched for a better shirt in her dresser drawer, she glanced out the window. She gasped.

Miss Grimm was placing her St. Jude statue on Lady's grave.

A tornado whirled inside Evi's stomach. She flew from the apartment, down the back stairs, into the yard, toward the grave. Her heart pounded.

"Take that statue off!" she screamed. "Lady's not a lost cause!"

Miss Grimm placed her hand on Evi's arm. Evi flung it off.

Miss Grimm's eyes were swollen and wet. "St. Jude is also the patron saint of lost souls," she said.

Evi clenched her fists. "I'm sick of your mean innuendoes," she shouted. "I *said* I was sorry about Lady! I'm *not* a lost soul! *You're* the lost soul!"

Evi ran to her building. Just as she reached the back door, Miss Grimm called out. "Evita! I didn't mean you. I meant Lady. I want St. Jude to guide my girl's soul into heaven. She'll be in heaven waiting for me, don't you think?"

Evi hesitated, her hand on the door knob. *I'll tell her now*, Evi decided. *I'll tell her I think prejudiced people don't get into heaven. I'll tell her I hate her and never want to talk to her again. I don't care if hating's a sin.*

Evi turned around.

Miss Grimm stood by the grave. Her shoulders drooped. Her watery eyes locked on Evi.

"Dogs need to run," Miss Grimm said. "Lady was always so peaceful after her outings with you."

Evi felt something thick fill her throat. She couldn't speak.

Jee

First published in *St. Anthony Messenger* (2011)

"MA! SPIDAH SPINNIN' web! C'mon look, Ma!"

Her son banged on her bedroom door, rattling the knob and shrieking about a spider. She was glad she'd remembered to lock the door. She wasn't ready for him. Right now she just couldn't deal with the energy of an 8-year-old boy.

"Mama's still sleeping, Kenny," Theolyn shouted.

She continued to sit cross-legged in the middle of her unmade bed, cleaning her brush. The hair gripped the brush, stubborn and sticky as cobwebs. She knew that Kenny's spider had put the unfortunate image in her head, where it would no doubt stay until she dyed her hair back to the brown it once had been. But why should she bother doing that? Who in her life cared that her hair looked cobwebby?

She sighed and yanked her hair from the brush, ignoring her son's escalating shrieks about a spider. She knew Kenny wasn't afraid of the spider. He wasn't afraid of anything. Perhaps it was his Down syndrome that inoculated him from fear and worry. He lived in the present. Except when he was having a tantrum, he smiled at everyone and everything.

He'd want her to catch the spider, put it in a jar, let him name it and feed it and try to teach it to crawl up and down his arms.

So many bugs had been loved to death by Kenny.

She'd been hoping for a few Kenny-free hours. She'd returned from her night shift at the nursing home to wonderful news.

"Kenny don't stay in the bed until after two o'clock in the morning," Gelmina had complained as soon as Theolyn walked in the door. Gelmina was the Lithuanian lady she paid $20 a night to sleep on her sofa while Kenny slept in his room down the hall.

"He must to watch *Ants* DVD five times. He don't sleep. I don't sleep. But now he sleep! Sun is up and now he sleep!"

"Sorry," Theolyn said, handing Gelmina an extra $5 for her trouble and ushering her out the door.

But Theolyn wasn't sorry at all. Kenny would sleep in! She'd be able to shower, drink a pot of coffee, and read the paper in peace. She wouldn't have to squander her Kenny-free time sleeping. What a lucky break that she'd been able to doze through some of her shift at the nursing home.

•

IT HAD BEEN a good shift. Only one resident had gotten out of bed and wandered into her office, agitated and garrulous. Theolyn had calmed the old man down the way she always did with her residents.

It was the same way she'd often soothed her agitated, elderly mother.

She'd sat the old man in a wheelchair next to her desk and brushed his sparse white hair, over and over, in long, gentle strokes, until he nodded off. Then she rolled him back to his bedroom. While he slept in the wheelchair, she sat on his bed, doing a crossword puzzle from a book on his nightstand. She finished a complete puzzle before an orderly answered her page and helped her get the old man back into bed.

Then she returned to her desk, started her paperwork, and when she found herself nodding off, she moved the monitor close and set the volume high so she'd be sure to hear if anyone cried out during the night.

•

BUT NOW SHE hadn't even read the paper yet, or showered, and there was Kenny, loud and demanding attention. Maybe Gelmina had exaggerated about how late Kenny had been up, angling for an extra tip. Kenny did not sound like a boy who'd been sleeping only a few hours.

"Ma!" Kenny pounded the door. "Open, Ma! Big spidah! Spidah wanna play!"

"Where's the spider, Kenny?"

"My woom! Big un, Ma! Open dooh! See!"

"Mama's busy, Kenny. Go away." She ripped more hair from the bristles.

Maybe today, if she could get Kenny down for a nap, she'd dash to Walgreens and buy a brand new hair brush, one that didn't remind her of Josiah every time she used it. She hated bringing Kenny into stores. He stuck things in his hands and under his clothes as stubbornly as the hair stuck in her brush.

Who was she kidding. She would never replace this brush. Nor would she ever leave Kenny alone at home.

It was gorgeous, the brush, and far more expensive than anything she'd find at Walgreens.

And it was the only thing, the only perfect thing, she had left of Josiah.

Josiah had given her the brush their one and only Valentine's together. The brush was polished wood, cherry, with a gold heart etched on the handle. She'd been hugely pregnant with Kenny then, full of happiness and hope and plans for a church wedding.

She'd get her wedding, Josiah had promised, as soon as she lost the baby weight.

Then Kenny was born, and a month later Josiah left. Just left. She and Kenny had returned from a long appointment at the pediatrician's. She'd known Josiah was gone as soon as she'd walked into their apartment. She'd felt his absence, smelled him gone, even before seeing their bedroom closet now holding only her clothes, even before opening the empty top dresser drawer which had once been crammed with his socks and underwear. Even before finding, under her pillow, the money order for $1,000.

He'd made it payable to her, Theolyn Molk. Not Timble, his last name. Legally, Timble hadn't belonged to her yet, but she'd signed their Christmas cards, The Timbles. She'd changed her library card to Theolyn Timble.

He'd taken everything important—his clothes, the iPod she'd given him their one and only Valentine's together, his last name.

On Kenny's fourth birthday, in a wine-fueled melancholy, she'd tossed into the trash everything that remained of Josiah: his bowling ball, a sterling silver heart necklace, Hallmark cards scrawled with his declarations of love.

She'd forgotten about the hair brush, though, and the next day, sober but still sad, she decided to keep it, to continue using it to rip through her shower-wet hair every morning, breaking through the snarls with punishing, painful strokes.

Once she'd hit Kenny with the brush. He was 6. He'd wet his pants again, worse this particular time because he'd been sitting on the couch watching a *Sponge Bob* cartoon. His urine had soaked the couch so thoroughly that, despite her subsequent spraying and scrubbing and drying, on rainy or humid days she could still smell the stink.

She'd whacked Kenny with the brush. Hard. On his bottom. He'd sobbed. She'd screamed.

But he hadn't wet himself since, and he was now 8 years old.

So even a Kenny could learn.

"Ma!" Kenny wailed. "Want spidah down! Get now!"

She inspected her now hair-free brush. Would he ever outgrow his love of bugs? Eight years old, but as fascinated with the bugs he dug up in the park as a toddler was. But even toddlers avoided him. She feared that Kenny would probably be fascinated with bugs when he was old and wrinkled, assuming he lived that long.

There was a hole in his heart, a ventricular septal defect that the cardiologist at Kenny's last checkup had heard through her stethoscope, but had struggled to see on the echocardiogram.

"It's getting smaller!" the doctor had said to Theolyn. "Less than two millimeters! Kenny may be one of the lucky ones whose VSD may yet close spontaneously. That almost never happens after age 4, but his is far enough away from the aortic valve that we can hold off on any surgery and hope it closes up in the next year or two. You must be saying your prayers!"

Theolyn smiled and nodded so that the doctor would think she was happy. She had been saying her prayers, of course. Hadn't she once been a postulant in the Third Order of the Sisters of St. Joseph?

She'd entered the convent after her mother finally died, freeing her from the endless grind of meds, insulin shots, meals, baths, laundry, doctors, walks, rosaries, and monologues—the same stories over and over and over.

She'd never taken her final vows, though. At age 40, she'd met Josiah. He was the driver for the Order's School on Wheels bus that traveled to the Spanish neighborhoods every day so that the nuns could help immigrants learn English.

So she'd smiled and nodded as the cardiologist talked and enthused that Kenny would likely enjoy a nice, long life. The cardiologist hugged Kenny. Theolyn did, too.

Of course she'd been saying her prayers, as had Kenny. She'd taught him. He could stumble through most of them, though only she, and possibly God, could understand his words.

But whose prayers was God choosing to refuse?

Hers, apparently.

•

"MA! OPEN WIGHT now!" Kenny banged the door hard. She heard wood crack.

She shot from the bed, gripping the brush, flinging open the door. Kenny was hopping and laughing. "Spidah! Get!"

"God bless it!" she screamed.

He froze. His mouth opened and his tongue drooped over his lower lip.

"Kenny! Bad boy! Look what you did!" She grabbed his hand and pressed it over the crack he'd made in the hollow pine door. She raised her arm and slammed the brush, hard. Her fingers vibrated from the impact, and for a moment she though the brush itself had splintered. But no.

The door. She'd hit the door, not Kenny. And there was now a second crack in the door.

Her stomach churned. "Dear Jesus," she said. "What did I almost do?"

Kenny clapped his hands. "Ma! Kenny sowwy!" He fell to his knees and began to pray. "Deah Jee. Sowwy Kenny hut dooh. Bad Kenny. Sowwy, Jee."

Theolyn sighed. She felt her anger leaking out as though Kenny's prayer had punctured her skin, letting the poisonous emotion whoosh away.

She crouched next to her son.

"It's Jesus, Kenny. Not Jee. Say Jee – zuz. Let's practice. Not Jee. Say Jee – zuz."

"Jee!" he shrieked. He smiled at her. His narrow eyes crinkled. His squat, freckled nose flared. There was nothing of his father's reckless, lupine face in Kenny. Down syndrome children all looked the same. Kenny's face would never reflect her own features, or Josiah's. And though Kenny would never remind her of Josiah, which was a blessing, neither would he ever tempt Josiah back to her. Josiah would have no curiosity about how his son was growing or looking. There'd be no Little League games for Josiah to yearn for, no driving lessons to sweat through, no first dates to admire, no pride in how his son was echoing the athleticism or charm or smarts of the old man.

There'd be no late night calls to Theolyn begging to hear how their boy was turning out.

•

"BWUSH HAY, MA." Kenny pulled her arm. "Sit," he ordered.

She sat cross-legged on the carpet. He sat next to her, but when she started to brush his hair, he shrieked. "No! Me!" She sighed and handed him the brush, but to her surprise, instead of pushing it through his own hair, he began to brush hers.

She closed her eyes and let the brush pull and stroke and massage her scalp.

"Gee, that feels nice, Kenny," she murmured.

Kenny giggled. "Not Jee, Ma. Jesus, Mama. Say Jesus."

Her eyes snapped open. She turned and faced her son.

He was smiling, murmuring "Jesus, Mama," over and over, and now plowing her brush through his own hair.

"Hug, Kenny," she whispered. He tossed the brush and flopped into her lap. She stroked his back. "Good boy, Kenny. You said it right for Mama. Jesus."

The brush had landed just beyond her reach, but she could see that it now held both their hair, her cobwebby gray and his silky brown.

Maybe she would dye her hair back to its youthful color. Match Kenny's. He had nice hair, soft and brown as cream-enriched coffee.

Kenny's thumb slipped into his mouth. He closed his eyes, smacking his thumb. He rested his head against her heart.

Her lower back was starting to throb from sitting on the floor, supporting her son who seemed to be melting into her. She could feel her right leg tingle from her son's weight.

She'd have to find the spider, she knew.

But not just yet.

Keeping Score
First published in *Woman's World* (2008)

RAMONA HART WAS 44, eleven years older than the man who wanted to marry her.

But he didn't know that.

They'd met four months ago over a Scrabble board. Ray ran a Scrabble Club for the park district. He had auburn hair, sunny blue eyes, and a laugh that made everyone smile.

Ramona joined the Scrabble Club because she had to fill up her time. Until she turned 44, her bakery job, her home and her marriage had kept her busy and happy. But then her husband of 20 years moved out of the home he shared with Ramona and into his young paralegal's apartment.

Ramona knew it would be easier to find a new pastime than to find someone new to love, so when she saw an item in her local paper advertising a weekly Scrabble Club, she decided to check it out. The following Saturday, she went. Players sat at long tables, drinking coffee and clicking letter tiles on Scrabble boards.

A tall man approached with a clipboard.

"Welcome! I'm Ray Lampman. We're always happy to see new players!"

She signed the clipboard, and then, because there weren't any available players, he offered to play a game with her.

"You be the scorekeeper, OK?" he asked. "Numbers aren't really my thing."

They talked as they played. She learned he taught high school English and was recently divorced.

"It's not easy starting over," he confessed. "Especially at this age. I'm 33."

Ramona didn't *exactly* lie. "I feel old. My husband moved into his 24-year-old girlfriend's apartment. Our divorce will be final next month."

"You don't look old," Ray said. "Mid-thirties?"

She shook her head. "A bit higher."

"Thirty-nine?"

She smiled. "You're good."

Later, she told herself that she'd meant he was good to place her at 39, not that he was accurate.

But now, five months later, sitting across from him in their favorite restaurant, she stared wordlessly at the diamond ring in a velvet box. Heat steamed her eyes.

"Maybe this is too quick?" Ray asked. "We've only known each other 153 days."

"Oh!" she gasped. She smiled despite her anxiety. "And you say you're not good with numbers!"

"Ramona," he said. "These days have been the most amazing of my life. But you need time. I understand. Just don't say no, not tonight. Let me hope. Let me try to help you say yes."

"Oh, Ray! I do love you. I love your mind and your heart and your blue eyes. And your beautiful laugh. It's just that, well, I'm older than you."

He laughed. Other diners looked at them, smiling.

"Ramona! It's only six years!"

"But you'd have a better chance having a family if you were with a younger woman."

"Oh sweetheart. These days plenty of women have children in their early forties. And I want to marry *you*. If we're not blessed with children, so be it."

She sighed. "I'm not exactly in my early forties."

He blushed. "I know. You're only 39. But age is just a number. Age has nothing to do with your green eyes, your warm heart, and your decency."

"I'm not decent!" she whispered.

He smiled. "Well, not when you shouldn't be."

"Ray, I'm. . ." She couldn't tell him. Instead, she opened her purse, removed her driver's license, and handed it to him.

He glanced at it. Laughed. "Well, nobody looks good in their license photo."

"Ray!" She stood. "I know numbers aren't your thing, but do the math!" And she fled to the restroom.

She sobbed behind the closed door of a stall. Finally, despite her flushed face and swollen eyes, she returned to their table.

He was gone. So was her purse. Her after-dinner cocktail was all that remained on the table.

The waiter approached. "The gentleman has taken care of the bill," he said. "But please, enjoy your drink."

"My. . .my purse?" she stuttered.

"It's safe with the maître d'." The waiter bowed and backed away.

Ramona slugged down her drink. She retrieved her purse from the maître d', and left.

They'd walked to the restaurant. It was only a mile from her house. She was grateful for the darkness as she walked home. No one would see her tears.

When she reached her house, she opened her purse, fumbled for her keys. Her fingers closed around a velvet box.

She pulled it out, opened it up. The diamond ring glistened under her porch light. A folded square of paper filled the lid. She unfolded it.

"I love you, Ramona," she read aloud. "I meant it when I said age is just a number. Fifty-four is a fine number. I love 54. I love you."

"Fifty-four?" Ramona whispered. Her heart fluttered. She hurried inside, called him on his cell.

"Hey you," he answered.

"Ray. I found the ring. I read your note."

"I mean it, Ramona. I'm sorry I left the restaurant, but you needed time to think."

"Ray, I know math is not your thing, but come on. If you subtract my birth year from this year, you get 44, not 54."

There was a long pause.

"Ray?"

"Will you marry me, Ramona?"

"You still wanted to marry me even when you thought I was 54?"

"Age is just a number, Ramona. I love you no matter what number you are."

Ramona smiled. "Ray," she said. "Come on over."

Lola
First published in *Woman's World* (2014)

"LOLA, LOLA, COME here sweet girl."

My eyes snapped open. It was my husband's voice I was hearing. He lay next to me in our moonlit bedroom. I sat up. The clock on my nightstand showed it was just after two a.m. I looked at Phil.

"Lola," he murmured again. His eyes were closed. He sighed.

He was dreaming. Not a problem. Except my name wasn't Lola.

That *was* a problem. And it couldn't have come at a worse time.

We'd been married 12 years. Our 13th wedding anniversary was Sunday, five days away. I'd made reservations at the Italian restaurant where he'd proposed. I'd bought him a watch, knitted him a sweater in light blue, his favorite color.

Was he actually having an affair with a woman named Lola?

At breakfast he was cheerful as always, gulped his coffee, grabbed his briefcase and a carrot muffin, and kissed me before leaving for work.

"Gotta work late tonight, Brie," he said. "Don't do dinner for me."

My head nodded. My lips smiled. My stomach ached.

It was later, doing laundry, when I found blonde hairs on his red sweater.

My hair is brown. Phil's hair is black.

Were these blonde hairs Lola's?

I drove in a daze to the bakery where I worked decorating cakes. My eyes burned with every buttercream flower I swirled on a customer's wedding cake.

I left work early, drove to Phil's office, parked across the street, watched him leave at five p.m. (so much for working late), and followed him six miles to a white frame house. I watched him ring the bell. I watched the door open. A woman, slim, in jeans and a green tee shirt, stood in the doorway.

They talked. Whatever Phil was saying made her happy. She hugged my husband, pulled him inside.

The door closed.

Was her hair blonde? I couldn't tell. She'd been wearing a kerchief. I waited a while longer. Then I drove back home.

Sunday came. I gave Phil the watch and sweater.

I had one more gift for him, but now I didn't know how I could give it to him. Not without crying. I waited for him to bring out whatever gift he'd gotten me.

"Brie," he said. "I know we've always said that important decisions should be made together."

My head nodded. My lips smiled. My stomach ached.

"We've been married 13 years today. For the 13th anniversary, the traditional gift is lace, but the modern gift is fur. I went ahead and I made an important decision without running it by you first."

So he'd gotten me an expensive fur coat, I thought. So he'd maxed out our credit card. A guilt gift to ease his conscience over his cheating on me with the golden-haired Lola.

He glanced at his new watch. Frowned. "Should be here any minute."

The doorbell rang.

On the doorstep stood the slim woman I'd seen Phil hug at the white frame house.

Her hair was red and curly.

She held a leash. Attached to the leash was a dog. A golden retriever.

"Lola, Lola, come here sweet girl," Phil said.

The dog bounded inside, jumped on Phil's legs.

"Happy anniversary, darling Brie."

"She's completely housebroken and trained," the woman said. "I've raised her since birth. She's a great dog. I had five dogs ready to be adopted, and your husband had a hard time deciding which one. But Lola decided for him. She never left his side whenever he visited."

I knelt before my new dog, ran my hands over her thick, beautiful, blonde fur.

"Is she good with kids?" I asked. My head was nodding. My lips were smiling. My stomach felt great.

"Absolutely," the woman said. "But Phil never mentioned you had children."

Phil was staring at me. "We don't," he said.

I laughed as Lola licked my face. "I've got one more gift for you," I said to Phil. "One we've been wanting for a long time."

Lola seemed to know before Phil did. She gently pressed her nose against my stomach.

I looked up at Phil. "Happy anniversary, Papa-to-be," I murmured.

The red-haired woman smiled. Lola barked. Phil sank to the floor. He opened his arms, and both Lola and I fit inside his hug just fine.

A Matter of School Pride
First published in *Storyteller* (2009)

THE GIRL STANDING on my front porch looked vaguely familiar, but she had a bruised eye, and when she smiled, I saw that one front tooth was whiter than the other. It was not quite flush with her other teeth, like an implant or a laminate not perfectly fitted.

"Is Jason home, Mrs. Warren?"

The phone was ringing, but my housekeeper hadn't left yet. She would answer it, and she knew what to say if it were my ex-husband again. So I could give my attention to this disturbing girl.

For there was something about her that frightened me.

"Jason has the baseball game after school today, honey. It's the quarterfinals for state."

"Oh! Right." The girl's unbruised eye, a pleasing sky blue, turned in just a bit toward her nose before righting itself again. My own drifting eye had been corrected decades ago, when I was much younger than this girl, who looked about 17, my son's age. I felt a brief pinch of annoyance at this girl's parents. In a well-off community like ours, there was no excuse not to fix that sort of flaw.

The girl sighed. "Jason . . . oh. Well. OK. Thanks."

She turned to go. I wondered how she could have forgotten about the game. The whole town was abuzz with excitement. I should have been at the game now, sitting in the lower stands behind home plate or by first base with the other starters' parents, but Jason had warned me.

Jason's father would be there, too.

A Matter of School Pride

I knew my ex-husband would sit in his usual spot right behind home plate, his big body made even bigger by the Stetson hat he always wore, blocking the sight lines of those behind him.

He'd be pumping his fist into the air, shouting instructions and opinions, until the Coach or umpire ordered him out of range.

•

"BUT I WANT you there, too, Mama-girl," Jason had said to me this morning before he'd left for school.

I'd shaken my head. "Not if your dad is going to be there."

Two pink spots had flared in Jason's cheeks. Without saying goodbye, he'd hefted his backpack and kicked open the back door with such force I heard the wood crack again.

I counted to 20, giving him time to cool down, then hurried out to the deck.

He was backing out of the garage. It was a warm spring morning, and the Mustang's top was down.

"Jason!"

He shifted into park but left the engine running. He stared up at me, 10 years old again with his red hair tousled and his height folded into the car and his glasses sliding down his freckled nose.

"Got your contact lenses?" I asked, though I knew he kept a supply in his baseball locker at school.

Jason muttered something and shifted into drive, but I called out again, and he braked. He looked at me, his face so blank he could have been sleeping but for the open, blinking eyes.

I smiled, fisted my hands, crossed them over my heart. After a moment, he signed "love" back to me, as crisply as a soldier's salute. Then he interlocked his index fingers once and repeated the motion in reverse.

"Friend," I signed back, and at last, he smiled. His eyes crinkled. Dimples sweetened his face. The ice in my throat melted. He waved and roared away, my little Cub Scout, his chubby little fingers flying through all the sign language I was teaching my scouts, my Jason learning faster than any of the other little boys in my pack, just yesterday, so many years ago.

•

THE GIRL WALKED carefully down our front porch steps, gripping the rail like a frail old lady. From behind my glass storm door, I watched her limp down our walkway.

"Goodbye!" I called out.

Then my hand grabbed the door knob. My arm pushed the door open, and my legs stumbled after her.

"Wait," I whispered, but she kept walking.

Suddenly, the name came to me.

Carly.

Cute little Carly in a darling lilac dress with fringe on the hem, spaghetti straps, her arms goosebumped in my air-conditioned Lexus as I drove her and Jason to homecoming two years ago, and I saw in the rearview mirror how he put his arm around her and rubbed warmth into her. I heard him scold her for not bringing the green shawl he'd bought her. It would've matched his green suit coat, he reminded her, which was the color of the school's sports teams and the best color for his red hair (my red hair too!).

As he talked, his eyes crinkled just like mine do when we smile, and my heart swelled with love for them both, though I dared not say a word. I would not emerge from chauffeuring-parent invisibility. I would not let them know, two 15-year-olds, that I saw, and I listened, and I was charmed.

When they scrambled from the Lexus, Carly tripped in her high-heeled sandals. Jason laughed and caught her arm.

"My clumsy little kitten," he said.

Though cars were lining up behind me, I couldn't leave just yet.

I gazed upon my handsome son and his pretty girl. They stood at the curb, Carly not even reaching his shoulder despite her high-heeled sandals and hair puffed up in soft brown curls. Jason whispered into Carly's ear. She straightened her shoulders. In front of them, silks and suits floated along a wide curving walkway into the glass and steel set far back. Every window on the school was lit green and glittering like square-cut emeralds. Balloons and streamers throbbed from trees, bushes, lamp poles.

It was the community's pride, this high school.

A Matter of School Pride

People put their names on realtors' waiting lists, moved here, and paid the high property taxes just to give their children the opportunity to attend.

"Hey, Jason!" Someone called out his name. Heads turned. Guys waved. Girls smiled and tossed their hair. "Jason! Jason!" Again and again his name punctured through laughter, chatter, idling car engines.

Jason lifted Carly's arm and waved it back to his friends.

Cars behind me began to beep, and I saw, in the sinking spray of sunlight, that Carly's arm, the one he'd rubbed warm the whole ride over, glowed with the imprint of four fingers. They curved like a bracelet over her white skin, but the red was already fading as I called out "goodbye-have-fun" and drove away.

I hadn't seen Carly since that night, though I knew they'd dated off and on over the past two years. Jason would casually mention a movie he'd seen with her, or that they'd studied for a test at her house. But he'd never brought her over to our home.

•

"CARLY!" I CALLED out. "Wait!"

From the end of our paved Italian brick walkway, she turned her bruised eye to me. And God help me, I asked her.

"How'd you get that shiner?"

She looked down. Her shoulders twitched.

I went to her, though I had no shoes, and the rough olive green brick of the walkway, which I hated and had never wanted, bit into the soles of my feet.

I put my arm around her, lightly. She smelled like the Absorbine Junior that Jason sometimes used on his aching muscles.

Something hard filled my throat. I led her back to the house.

•

LATER, TOGETHER, NOT sipping the tea which my housekeeper had served, we both watched and waited for the man to react to what Carly and I had stuttered out.

The man sat at my kitchen table across from Carly and me. He reached for a second cookie. They were chocolate chip with macadamia nuts, Jason's favorite, baked by me just that morning.

The game had ended an hour earlier. Jason had texted me. He'd hit a grand slam. We'd won. He wouldn't be home for a while. The team was celebrating with pizza and bowling.

The man at my kitchen table chewed and swallowed. He had thin eyes, a pleasing sky blue color. He wore a green polo shirt. The high school's mascot, a lion, was embroidered under the collar over the words *Assistant Varsity Baseball Coach*.

He sighed, shook his head, drummed manicured fingers on the table top. No wedding band, but the high school's green-stone ring squeezed his right ring finger.

"Did ya know my sophomore son is sometimes moved up to varsity?" he asked me. "He doesn't get off the bench much when he plays varsity, but he's thrilled just to have his occasional shot at wearing the varsity jersey. This school's team is going places, thanks to your son, Mrs. Warren."

I nodded, felt pride heat my face.

Jason was the varsity team's leadoff batter and ace pitcher. He could throw 92 miles an hour, and his curves were unhittable. Semifinals were next. Then playoffs for state. Maybe 10 more days of baseball. Maybe two weeks.

We all expected the school to win.

The man at my kitchen table eating my cookies looked at me, then Carly.

Carly flinched. I wanted to put my arms around her, but that was no longer my role.

"Here's what we do," he said.

I shivered. Goosebumps stabbed my arms. Carly lifted her tea cup. Her hand shook, and tea splashed into her lap. She set the cup down without drinking.

"Let's wait for the trophies before we distract Jason," he said. He cleared his throat. "It's a matter of school pride."

The tension that had been squeezing my ribs snapped. My throat released a sigh, and my heart began to beat normally again.

A tiny sound, like a kitten's squeak, came from Carly.

"Can I drive you home, honey?" he asked Carly. "I'm gonna head over to the bowling alley where the team's celebrating, but I can drop you home first."

Carly looked down at her tea. "No thanks. I'll walk home, Dad."

He nodded. I walked him to the front door. He held out his hand. I shook it. The high school ring on his finger pressed into my skin.

He sighed. "Well, Mrs. Warren. I appreciate you calling me. I know it had to be hard. But Jason is a fine young man. He's been a great mentor for my son. Treats him good, not like some of the other varsity players, those who sit on the bench a little too much. Those guys resent my boy. Don't talk to him, don't high-five when he scores. But Jason's not that way. He even let my son use his bat, and I know how territorial players can be about their bats. OK, Jason made a mistake with Carly. But that aggression, it's part of what makes a good athlete. I know we can straighten out this situation. I'll be happy to talk to him for you. After the season ends. I don't think this needs to go beyond the two of us.

I nodded, pushed my lips into a smile so wide my cheeks ached.

I watched him drive away in his green Hummer.

I returned to the kitchen. Carly was holding a cookie. She saw me and set it back on the platter.

"Would you like to take some home, honey?" I asked. "I can put as many as you want in a bag. I didn't know you had a younger brother. He must be a talented baseball player if he sometimes plays varsity. I bet he'll enjoy a few tonight."

She nodded. "Sure, Mrs. Warren. Thanks."

I wanted her gone. I wanted my Jason home. I wanted to hear his side of the story. There are always two sides. He'd explain it all. Everything would be fine once Jason explained.

I rummaged in the cabinet for a Ziploc bag. "You know, honey," I said to Carly, who was standing so close behind me I could feel her breath, "your dad will take care of things for you. He seems like a good guy."

"I look like my mom," Carly said. "Everyone says."

"Oh?" It was all I could think to respond. What a strange thing to say right now, I thought. I began piling cookies into the Ziploc bag.

"She's living in Reno now. Remarried. To my Dad's best friend." She laughed. "Well, ex-best friend, I guess."

I froze. "Oh," I whispered, suddenly understanding. She had no one. No advocate. Cookies overfilled the bag. I forced the seal closed, smashing some of the cookies. "I'm sorry." I wasn't sure what I was apologizing for.

She took the bag. I followed her to the front door, watched her walk down the steps, gripping the railing like a frail old lady. I watched her limp down the walkway.

"Goodbye!" I called out.

"Wait," I whispered.

I ran after her.

"Please, Carly." I put my arm around her, lightly. She looked up at me, so tiny she didn't even reach my shoulder.

"Come back to the house."

She blinked, stepped away from me. "For what?" She started to shake. The bag of cookies fell to the sidewalk.

My heart hammered. Something hot pressed behind my eyes. *Tell her goodbye*, I told myself. *Let Jason explain, set things right.*

I knew Jason would grab my hands. He'd look at me straight, his eyes wide, maybe misting just a bit. He'd stutter, just a bit. He'd tremble. He'd promise. Like his dad.

And I'd forgive him. Like I always used to forgive his dad. We'd hug. We'd both cry.

I wasn't responsible for Carly. That was her dad's job. But I knew what her dad would do. He'd encourage her to get over it. He'd tell her he'd give Jason a stern lecture about saving his aggression for the team. He'd tell her everything was now fine, would continue to be fine. No one had really gotten really hurt. Jason wouldn't do it again.

She'd believe. Like I always had. It was always easier to believe.

Until it wasn't.

I looked at Carly's bruised eye.

"I'm calling the police." My voice shook. I didn't have the strength to fix my son. But others would. Wouldn't they? *Oh God, please. Let this be the right thing I'm doing.*

We both looked down at the bag of broken cookies.

"But the playoffs," she whispered. She bit her lower lip.

I shook my head. "I have to do this now. *Me*. Because Jason is *my* son. And I love him. I'm doing this because I love him."

"No! I don't want to! I just want to go home now!" Her eyes glistened. She began to walk away.

I called her name.

She stopped, turned to face me.

I bent down and grabbed the bag of cookies, but when I straightened up, I suddenly felt dizzy. I staggered, the cookies fell again, and she ran to me. I gripped her shoulders to keep from falling.

"Mrs. Warren? Are you OK?" She draped my arm over her tiny shoulders, and though I felt my whole weight press down, she stayed upright. She kept me from falling.

"No, Mrs. Warren," she said. "It could hurt the team."

I closed my eyes, and saw my little Cub Scout. My sweet little boy. I opened my eyes and looked at Carly. "We have to," I said. "It's a matter of school pride."

Again she bit her lower lip.

"My pride, too," I whispered. "And yours."

I waited.

At last, she nodded.

Together we returned to the house.

Mucked
First published in *Storyteller* and *Writer's Digest* (2007)

I GET BORED. It's the downside to being born into wealth, good looks, natural athleticism, and intelligence. Everything comes too easy, so I have to manufacture drama and challenges.

That's why I love poker. But poker without deception is boring. And cheating is the purest deception, better than bluffing. Yet, cheating is only thrilling against the right opponents.

So when my real estate gal told me about the co-op coming on the market in Salmon Towers, I moved fast. It's not that I wanted a view of Lake Michigan and the Chicago skyline. What I wanted was the poker games the Salmon is secretly famous for. Problem was, you had to live in the Salmon to hook an invite.

Three million dollars and three co-op board interviews later, I was in.

Now the fun could begin.

•

FIVE OF US sat in Zabu's den, 20 stories over Lake Shore Drive. The table was round, the lamp hung low, and smoke curled from our cigarettes, even mine, though I detest the filthy habit. But I'd coated my cigs with my own special formula. Touching the cig transferred the chemical to my finger. Touching the card transferred the chemical to the card. Soon, I'd managed to mark most of the cards. The daubs were visible only to me, courtesy of my special glasses. They were scholarly wire rims, with lenses thin as a fashion model and "clear" as a politician's conscience.

For a while I played cautious, folding when I knew I didn't have to, letting myself get bluffed out of the pot when I knew I could safely call. I was happily sizzling with fear. Get caught cheating by the four specimens sitting around Zabu's table, and money would never buy me love again.

But I hadn't bought the apartment across the hall from Zabu to play nice.

Zabu dealt me two red sevens. When I peeked at those hockey sticks, I knew the time had come to skate loose.

The flop flipped three low clubs, non-consecutive. The daubs I'd marked on the cards showed that only Zabu had backdoor flush potential. He held the Ace of clubs and a red six.

Kamel, Inashima, and McCroquodale checked, I bet, and Zabu raised, big time. Clearly he was bluffing that he'd already made the flush.

McCroquodale and I called. Zabu looked at us. A smile lurked around his thin blue eyes. The turn displayed a red Queen, giving McCroquodale a pair, the best hand pre-river, though only I knew that.

The river exposed a beautiful red six. I checked. Zabu lasered his thin eyes at me, and went all in.

McCroquodale folded his winning lady, convinced Zabu had the flush.

Butterflies, moths, vampire bats all flapped their wings inside my gut. Was now the moment to risk Zabu's wrath? An angry loser is a suspicious loser. The pot was luscious—100 grand.

I went all in.

Zabu didn't blink, but as his chips hemorrhaged to me, color drained from his face.

McCroquodale sipped his whiskey sour. Kamel lit another cig. Inashima played with the diamond stud in his ear.

Zabu curled his lips into a snaky smile. "Why you stay in with two hockey sticks?" he asked. "You must to know something you cannot know, unless you a cheatbagging, scum-sucking, bottom feeder."

"Instinct, big Z," I said, curling my own lips into a snaky smile. "My instinct said you were bluffing. And I could see your left eyelid twitching."

My toes twitched. Sweat flooded my armpits. *Ay caramba*, this was poker at its finest.

Zabu touched his left eyelid. "My eyelid don't twitch."

I shrugged, stacked his chips, my chips now, into neat towers.

"You must to have pretty good eyeballs to see what not there," he said. Then he lunged over the table and yanked off my specs.

"I can't see the cards without my glasses," I remarked with complete honesty.

"So squint," Zabu said. He propped my glasses over his big nose. His lips moved as he studied the cards, seeing the spots I'd marked like a clock.

He smiled at me. "You, my friend, are mucked."

•

I DON'T GET bored anymore. I don't have to manufacture drama and challenges. These days, just crossing a busy street is thrilling.

I still play poker. And though my opponents are all quite nice, the games are slow. It takes time for each of us to feel the braille bumps on the cards.

Next
First published in *Storyteller* (2009)

GRIPPED BETWEEN HER two bodyguards, Ava was hurtled through the doors of the recording studio and into Hollywood's electrified night. Cameras swarmed, boisterous and bold. Bulbs flashed, scorching her skin.

Like a thousand bee stings, Ava thought.

She'd been stung once, not by a thousand bees, maybe just a dozen, and they'd been wasps, not bees, but the pain she was feeling now from the cameras' assault was the same. Snips, pinches, and prickles, hot and itchy, on her face, neck, mostly bare bosom, and naked arms.

How could she have once welcomed that heat? When had she stopped flourishing in that warmth?

Now the ice below her skin never seemed to melt. If she had a knife, she could peel her skin; then she could welcome the cameras' flash, let the cameras heat her frozen blood so it could flow again.

But there were always people around, watching her, keeping her voice safe, her sales hot, the money flowing.

She longed to yank her arms from the painful grip of her bodyguards as they hauled her to the waiting limousine. She felt the soreness of a zit on her chin, which her makeup man had disguised with concealer. She wanted to scratch off the concealer. She wanted to scrape at the zit until it bled.

She needed her arms freed.

Do I have the strength to break free? she wondered.

Her arms were firm, muscles toned by expensive hours in expensive gyms. She'd never suffered flab. Not even after giving birth to twin girls. Her arms had stayed firm then, too, from pushing strollers and lifting babies.

A lifetime ago. Six years ago.

•

THEY'D BEEN AT the zoo near their Chicago apartment, by the polar bear grotto, Ava and her 9-month old twins. It was hot but comfortable under the shade of a box elder. She watched the big white polar bear swim gracefully back and forth past the underwater viewing window. Teqila and Tomassa dozed next to her in the double stroller.

Ava sipped her icy Coke and smiled at the bear. She didn't notice the gray-brown nest hanging like a brittle, papery top from a branch over her head.

The wasps attacked. She flung a blanket over her babies before flailing her arms, fighting the wasps, sweeping them off her skin, smashing some in her bare hands.

Later, she and Emmanuel counted 12 welts on her neck, arms, and face.

But not one on her babies.

That had been a lifetime ago, when she'd been safely anonymous, a new bride and a new mother, needing only herself, her new husband, and her anonymity for protection.

A lifetime ago. Before she'd won their local park district talent contest, just her luck that a producer had been sitting on a folding chair in the front row of the gym, there to listen to his niece sing.

How impressed he'd been with Ava's buttery perfect pitch as she sang *Over the Rainbow*. He'd put Ava on his TV talent show. She'd survived all the elimination rounds.

She'd won, as Emmanuel put it, *the whole caboodle*.

But she'd lost her family.

Emmanuel refused to follow her to Hollywood. The celebrity life, he said, was not for him or their precious babies. The celebrity life, he said, was toxic, like a cancer, and by God he wasn't going to let it infect their little girls.

She gave him his divorce. She gave him her babies. A small price to pay, she thought at the time, for fame, fortune, fans, fun.

She was young. She could sing. Make-up artists and hair stylists made her lovely.

Diapers, drafty apartments, and devil wasps were easy to give up.

But she got older. Ancient in the celebrity world. Six years of flings and photo shoots and frenemies. Six years of drugs and detox and Botox.

Now she knew.

What were a few wasps compared to the assaults she now endured?

•

THE BODYGUARDS THRUST her into the limo. The limo pushed through cameras and shouts and shrieks and sped along Hollywood Boulevard.

They pulled up to a record store, and again she endured a gauntlet of cameras and fans as she was hustled into the store.

She sat behind a table, signing her new CD for a long line of mostly teenage girls and their mothers.

"Next!" barked her bodyguard.

The next person in line crouched over two little girls, his back to Ava. He was smoothing their black hair.

"Come on, buddy!" the bodyguard yelled. "You're next!"

The man stood and turned.

Ava gasped.

His little girls grabbed his legs. They stared at Ava, their eyes shiny and dark.

"Sorry, sorry," Emmanuel stuttered. His posture drooped, like an old man's. His face was flushed. His eyes were wet. "It's what they wanted for their birthday. They're 7 next week, you know. They love your songs."

They approached, the little girls mostly hiding behind his legs, peeking up at her, not smiling, looking frightened. One of them—Tomassa?—shook her head, frowned. Emmanuel gently placed two of Ava's CDs on the table.

"Don't worry," he murmured. "Their mother, they know she's gone."

"Gone?" Ava whispered. She could not stop looking at her babies.

"I . . . I thought it was for the best," Emmanuel said. "Them thinking that . . ."

"Chop, chop, buddy," the bodyguard said. "Line is long. Time is short."

Ava gazed at her little girls. How could she not know which one was which? Was it Tomassa or Teqila frowning at her?

"We drove 13 hours to get here," Emmanuel said.

Her hand shook as she scrawled her signature in permanent black marker over the photo of her smiling, blemish-free face.

The bodyguard grabbed the CDs and thrust them at Emmanuel.

"Next!" the bodyguard shouted.

Emmanuel hesitated.

"Excuse me!" The mother standing behind Emmanuel snapped her fingers. The mother's teenage daughter chewed gum and pointed her cell phone camera at Ava.

"It was your choice," Ava said to Emmanuel.

He straightened his shoulders. Now he stood tall. His eyes glittered. "You couldn't wait to give it to me," he replied.

They turned, Emmanuel and their little girls. They began walking away, past the throbbing, fat, snake of fans.

One of her daughters looked back over shoulder and stuck out her tongue.

Ava felt a blush heat her face. Tomassa. Even as babies, Tomassa had been the sassy one.

Ava scrawled her signature on the gum-chewing teen's CD. When she looked up, her family had disappeared.

"Next!" the bodyguard ordered.

Ava stood.

"Wait," she whispered.

Ava ran. She ignored her bodyguards' shouts. She flailed her arms against the hordes of fans reaching out for her, calling her name, snapping their cell phone cameras at her.

Ava ran and ran. She didn't know what would come next, but she knew what she was leaving, and it seemed to her as she spun through the store's revolving door and saw her family far away,

Next

nearly to the corner, it seemed to her as she raced after them, screaming "Wait!" and not caring whether she strained her vocal cords, it seemed to her as though the sweat shimmering her skin was finally soaking heat into her blood.

Quieting Lambent
First published in *St. Anthony Messenger* (2014)

THIS WAS SUPPOSED to be *my* birthday dinner at my favorite restaurant, but the Brat was ruining it. She was whining because my dad wouldn't let her have a sip of his wine.

"My mama lets me!" she shouted.

Brat is only 7 for God's sake. Dad wouldn't even let me have a sip, and today was my Sweet 16th.

"Dumbskull," Brat muttered, then she lunged for Dad's wine. He lifted it beyond her reach.

"Oops!" she yelled as her arm "accidentally" knocked her bowl of baked French Onion soup off the table. She insisted on "helping" our waiter clean the mess, and of course made a bigger mess, flinging soggy croutons from the soup back onto our table.

Later she complained loudly while we ate our porterhouse steaks and grilled asparagus. "I'm bored! I'm not hungry! This food stinks like puke! I want to watch TV at the bar!"

"Sweetheart," Dad said in his usual low, calm voice. "The bar's only for adults."

"Mama lets me!" she yelled.

Now she was screeching because she wanted more soup even though we had all finished our main course and were waiting for my birthday cheesecake. Diners at nearby tables gave us scorching looks. Dad promised to make soup for her when we got home, but she cried that she wanted soup NOW.

"Hey!" I stood and patted the big side pocket on my new pink sweater. "If you can guess what I have in my pocket, you can have it."

Brat stopped crying. She stared at my pocket. Dad's drooping mouth flipped into a spectacular smile—all for me.

For one blissfully quiet moment, I could pretend that it was just Dad and me again. No squalling, ferocious, foul-mouthed 7-year-old girl who was burning down the peaceful life Dad and I had enjoyed.

Until four weeks ago, when Brat erupted like a volcano into our lives.

Brat's actual name is Lambent.

"What kind of name is Lambent?" I asked her the day she arrived.

"Dunno." She kicked my leg.

Brat.

"It means glowing," Dad said as he dragged an air mattress for her into my bedroom.

Now I forced a smile at Brat. She kept staring at the pocket on my sweater. I buttoned the pocket—"Don't want it to fall out," I said—and sat back down.

Dad patted Brat's hand.

"Lambent," he said, "what do you think Marianne has in her pocket?"

Brat frowned. "Do you know?" she asked him.

"Not a clue," Dad said, "but"—he looked at me—"if *I* guess right, can I have it?"

I nodded. "Whoever guesses right, gets it. Here's the rules. You can ask questions about it before you make your guess, but my only answers are going to be yes, no, or sometimes. You can say what you think it is whenever you want. But!" I held up my forefinger just the way my mom used to do when we played this game. "You. Only. Get. ONE. Guess."

Brat's eyes glittered. When she wasn't pitching mayhem, her eyes were OK, the color of topaz. Not blue like Dad's and mine, but yellow-green like her mom's. Her mom was Drina, Dad's adopted sister. So Brat wasn't my *real* cousin. She'd been dumped on us when her mom got put in jail for selling look-alike drugs—fake crack and bogus Vicodin—to an undercover officer.

I'd never met Brat until she invaded us. She and her mom lived in a trailer park near Los Angeles, over 2,000 miles from our high-rise Chicago condo.

"Just until your Aunt Drina's problems get resolved," Dad had promised me. "We can't let Lambent go into the foster system. She's family."

She wasn't, I wanted to say. My mom wouldn't have let this happen. But Mom was gone. Cancer when I was 9.

"So how long will Aunt Drina be in jail?" I'd asked Dad the day we got the phone call about Brat needing a home.

He sighed. "I wish I knew," he said.

I soon knew it would be a long time. I'd listened in on the extension later that night when Dad was talking to some lawyer. Aunt Drina's bail had been set high, too high for Dad to pay *this* time.

So I figured there'd been other bails Dad had paid. Maybe those other bails were why he'd canceled our cruise last spring break.

This was Aunt Drina's third arrest. She'd stay in jail awaiting hearings and trial.

I'd met her only once. I was 8. She'd come to spend Thanksgiving week with us, skinny as a straw, sniffing and rubbing her nose except when she was crocheting.

She'd taught Mom to crochet rosaries. I remember snuggling between them on the sofa, watching their golden crochet hooks loop through soft yarn. Mom's plan was to sell the rosaries at my school's annual fundraising craft fair in the spring. By Thanksgiving morning, they'd crocheted enough rosaries to fill the crystal bowl on Mom's dresser.

"I like the bead rosaries better," I said to Mom as I fingered the yarn rosaries Thanksgiving night. "These are too quiet."

Mom laughed. "A quiet set of beads to quiet the mind," she said.

Two days after Thanksgiving, Aunt Drina left. After she left, Mom couldn't find her emerald necklace, her pearl and sapphire earrings, or the gold wedding ring that had belonged to her mom.

But all the rosaries were there. The cheap yarn rosaries made from the scraps Mom had left over from her knitting projects.

Mom never did sell them at my school's craft fair. She got sick after Christmas. All the long weeks when she was too weak to leave her bed, Dad and I and Mom would each select a yarn rosary from the crystal bowl on Mom's dresser, and we'd pray, taking turns leading each decade.

It was true. The quiet beads quieted my mind.

After Mom died, I got out of the rosary habit. Though Dad never moved the crystal bowl off Mom's dresser, I hadn't grabbed one out of there in a long time. Years. Our life was quiet and peaceful enough.

Until Brat.

In the four weeks Brat had been with us, we'd gone through three nannies. Brat had bitten, scratched, and kicked all three. She'd stolen money from one, car keys from another, and poured syrup over the third's laptop. She'd flushed our goldfish down the toilet, unraveled my half-knitted scarf when I was at summer school, and thrown my parents' framed wedding photo down the garbage chute. And this was despite her twice-weekly sessions with a therapist.

•

A TRIO OF waiters appeared at our table. One carried a bouquet of 16 helium-filled balloons in different pastel colors. Another set a Key Lime cheesecake in front of me, 16 candles blazing on top. The third played a guitar and sang happy birthday to me in a beautiful tenor voice.

Before I could blow out the candles, Brat lunged and blew them all out.

"Lambent!" Dad exclaimed. *Brat,* I thought.

"I'll light them again," the waiter offered.

I shook my head. "It's OK." I just wanted to get out of restaurant before Brat caused another scene.

The balloons were placed in the middle of our table. Long ribbons anchored them to a weighted pouch.

The waiter set fat slices of cheesecake in front of us. Dad and I dug in. Brat ignored hers. She looked from the balloons to me, then leaned close, trying to see the pocket on my sweater.

"Is it alive?" she asked.

I shook my head.

"Is it something you can eat?" Dad asked.

I shook my head.

"Is it soft?" Brat asked.

I nodded. "And pretty," I couldn't resist adding even as my stomach clenched. Maybe this game was a mistake. I was getting a little worried how it would end.

Because there was *nothing* in my pocket.

Brat coughed. "Is it something from my mama?"

I hesitated. "Yes," I said. Dad shot me a worried look. Brat gasped.

"Oh!" she murmured. She pushed her fists to her mouth. "Oh!" she murmured again.

My heart squirmed.

By the time we paid the check, we were still playing the game, but fortunately for my empty pocket, neither Brat nor Dad felt confident enough to risk their one guess.

We stood to leave the restaurant. Dad took Brat's hand. She pulled away from him and moved close to me.

"I want to hold Marianne's hand," she said. She looked up at me, smiling, her cheeks pink, her eyes bright and liquid.

She glowed.

Lambent.

I handed the balloons to Dad. I let Lambent wrap her hand into mine. I was surprised at how it felt, like I was holding a little bird.

We left the restaurant, Lambent asking questions, but still too unsure to risk her one guess.

We walked down the street to our car. Lambent's hand gripped mine. The balloons held by Dad swayed and bounced over us. Other pedestrians smiled at us. Some passing cars honked and their passengers sang out happy birthday.

I smiled and waved back, but I was feeling guilty. I'd tricked her, but I'd just wanted to quiet her down. And the game had worked. But now I'd have to trick her again. Find something soft and pretty when we got home, sneak it into my pocket, lie that it was from her mom.

The balloons filled our car's back seat, so the three of us sat in front. Lambent snuggled between us.

As we drove home, it hit me. Of course. The perfect thing to put in my pocket.

Maybe it was the colorful balloons whispering in the back seat as they rubbed together. Maybe it was Lambent snuggling between Dad and me in the car's front seat. Maybe it was because Lambent wasn't making her usual whiney noises, so I could think without distraction.

Whatever. Somehow my mind had flashed onto the perfect thing to put in my pocket. I'd just have to do it without Lambent seeing me.

Fortunately, by the time we got home, Lambent needed the bathroom. She'd probably drunk five glasses of pop at the restaurant. That gave me a chance to grab a rosary from the bowl on Mom's dresser.

Dad was at his desk in the den, reading work e-mails on his computer.

"Can you keep Lambent quiet a little while longer?" he asked me. "I've got a few things to do for work, then maybe we can all go the park, tire her out."

I held up the rosary. "We'll keep playing the guessing game. Aunt Drina made this one. This is what I'll put in my pocket."

"Ah." Dad smiled. "Thank you, sweetheart. That's a beautiful idea."

•

LAMBENT FOUND ME in the kitchen.

"Is it something I can wear?" she asked.

"Hmm," I said. My plan was to drag this out as long as possible.

She stared at the pocket, frowning. Then, suddenly, she rushed at me. It all happened so fast. She yanked at my pocket. The button flew off. She thrust her fist into the pocket.

"What?" She held the rosary up. "This isn't from Mama! You lied. I seen these stupid necklaces on the bowl on the dresser!" She kicked my leg. She flung the rosary to the floor.

I crouched and picked it up. I should have been furious. The button. My leg. But my leg didn't hurt much from where she'd kicked. And the button could be sewn back on. I cupped the rosary in my palm. So soft, so light. Like holding a little bird.

I stood, looked at Lambent. Her hands were clenched. Her face was twisted like a gargoyle.

"It *is* from your mama," I said. "She crocheted it with my mom a long time ago. Before you were born. I know it's hers because she was using this different colored yarn. And it's not a necklace, but I suppose you could wear it around your neck."

I placed it around her neck.

"Mama made this?" She fingered the beads—blues, greens, purples, yellows, pinks. Then rubbed the white yarn cross between her thumb and forefinger.

"It's called a rosary," I said. "People use it to pray. These are quiet beads to quiet the mind. When my mom was sick, we'd say special prayers on these rosaries. And it worked. I was sad and scared because my mom was going away soon, but when we prayed the rosary together, my mind got quiet."

Lambent gripped the rosary around her neck with both hands.

"So maybe," I said, "there are sad and scary feelings being loud in your mind? Like there were in mine?"

Lambent looked at the floor. She shuddered.

"I could teach you how to pray the rosary, Lambent. If you want. We could say it together."

She said nothing. All I could hear was the clock ticking on top of the refrigerator and Dad's low voice murmuring into the phone in the den.

Then she nodded.

Rosa
First Published as "A Tail of Grace" in *Liguorian* (2012)

EASTER SUNDAY AFTER church was as good a time as any for Lily to start boxing up her mother's things. No one was expecting Lily for Easter dinner.

Soon Lily would have to leave her mother's little house in Rantoul, Illinois, and return to her own condo and job 130 miles north in Chicago. She'd used up all her personal time-off days taking care of her mother after the stroke. The director of the year-round private school where Lily taught English and coached soccer had offered an unpaid leave of absence for as long as she needed, but Lily had bills to pay, and she missed her students.

Rosa, her mother's old dog, stretched out on the parlor rug, watching Lily sort clothes and books, papers and knickknacks. Since her mother's death, it seemed to Lily that Rosa was always watching her. The dog's watery brown eyes never left Lily's face. Was Rosa afraid, Lily wondered, to resume her frequent napping? Was the dog afraid Lily would disappear like her mother had?

Since Lily's mother had died, Rosa only closed her eyes at night, when Lily did.

"What am I going to do with you, sweetheart?" Lily asked.

Rosa thumped her tail.

"Who will take an old girl like you?"

Lily glanced at her own reflection in the mirrored wall behind the sofa. Her hair was still mostly brown, but lines bracketed her mouth and webbed the corners of her eyes. She looked her age, 37. She'd been 28 when her husband had left her for a 21-year-old hostess at a Chicago nightclub. Lily had started feeling like an old girl at 28.

"I'd take you if I could, Rosa. But my condo association says no dogs."

Rosa twitched her ears. She gazed at Lily without blinking. Lily looked away until the heaviness squeezing her heart eased.

"I've asked Mom's neighbors and friends, my friends and relatives. Well, everyone but Teddy. I don't know, Rosa. Could we trust Teddy to take care of you? He couldn't even manage to show up on time for Mom's funeral."

Lily shook her head, recalling how her brother had rushed into church during the eulogy, pulling his latest girlfriend behind him, both of them chewing gum and wearing flip-flops and jeans.

"Sorry," he'd whispered to Lily as he sat down next to her in the pew. "Rehearsals went late last night. I overslept."

•

"WELL, LET'S THINK about it, Rosa," Lily said.

Rosa sighed and thumped her tail. Lily continued to sort and box her mother's things. Whenever she looked up, she saw Rosa gazing at her. Her paws rested on the blanket that had covered Lily's mother during her last weeks. It was the blanket Lily had knitted in her high school home arts class. Now Rosa dragged the blanket everywhere. Occasionally, Rosa would thrust her nose in the blanket and breathe deeply. The blanket had become sticky from Rosa's drool, but Lily was reluctant to wash it. She didn't want to deprive Rosa of her mother's scent. Wherever Rosa went, Lily decided, her blanket would go, too.

Lily looked at the phone console next to her mother's rocking chair. "What the heck," she said.

She sat down in the rocking chair next to the phone. Her finger hovered over the button that would speed dial her brother's cell phone.

She said to Rosa, "I can't take you to a shelter. I just can't. You were such a faithful friend to Mom. I'll convince my brother to take you. I'll pay for everything. Heck, I'll pay him 100 bucks a month over expenses to take care of you. He'll take you, sweetheart. Don't you worry."

She let her finger drop and punch the button on the phone console. The phone rang. She pulled her mother's rosary from her sweater pocket and began fingering the beads, glad again that she'd removed the rosary from the casket. Since her mother's death, she'd resumed saying the rosary every night before bed, a habit she'd abandoned in college. Rosa would stretch out on the bed next to her. As Lily murmured the prayers, the dog would make her own throaty rumbles.

Now, waiting for her brother to answer the phone, Lily rubbed the rosary beads, and the butterflies in her stomach stopped fluttering.

"Hello?"

Her brother's voice was soft, sleepy, almost unrecognizable.

Lily started to sing. "Happy Easter to you, Happy Easter to you." To her surprise, he let her get all the way to the end without interruption. "Happy Easter Dear Brother, Happy Easter to you."

"Beautiful," he said. "You're a beautiful mezzo-soprano."

Her brother sounded different. Maybe, Lily decided, he was in character for some role. He was a part-time actor in Chicago area theater productions.

Lily felt tears warm her eyes. She couldn't remember the last time her brother had said anything nice to her. Maybe 20 years ago, when he'd whistled as she'd walked down the stairs dressed in a pink gown for her high school senior prom.

"You clean up nice, Little Sis," he'd said.

But five years later, at her wedding, he'd been a no-show. Their uncle had walked her up the aisle instead. She'd stumbled, her eyes burning from unshed tears.

Now Lily let her tears fall freely. "Thank you, Teddy."

"Teddy? I'm sorry. This isn't Teddy. My name is Travis. I take it Teddy is your brother?"

"Oh! I'm sorry! I thought you were my brother. You didn't sound much like him, but I thought—wait, I couldn't have dialed wrong. This number is programmed on my mom's speed dial."

But as she spoke, she realized that Teddy's number had been programmed a long time ago. Before moving back to Chicago last year, her brother had been hopping all over the country. Who knows how many times he'd changed his number? She'd given up calling him, finding e-mail a more reliable way to reach him. E-mail was how she'd let him know about their mother's stroke, and later, her death.

Travis was speaking. She pressed the phone to her ear. "Well, I've had this number for a week now. New cell phone, new number, new life."

"Oh brother. Teddy never bothered to tell me he changed it."

"Yes, you said he was your brother." He laughed. "Sorry for that goofy comment, but I'm still half-asleep. What time is it by you?"

"By me? In Illinois? It's one o'clock. In the afternoon."

"Ah. Now I must seem like a lazy bum, still sleeping, but I drove our motor home through the night. Now my son is driving. We hit a seven a.m. Easter Mass at a little church, jeesh, I forget where, and I'm sorry to say I dozed off during the sermon. We're probably somewhere in Georgia right now."

"Well, I'll let you get back to sleep. I'm sorry I bothered you."

"No, no, you didn't. I meant it when I said you're a beautiful mezzo-soprano. Thank you for the Easter greeting song. You have a nice vibrato, by the way."

Lily felt herself blush. "I do?" She looked down at the rosary pooled in her palm, the beads sapphire blue, heart-shaped.

"You do. I was the music director for my church for 20 years. I could've used a singer like you, especially after my wife died. She had a voice like yours, smooth and warm."

Lily felt her heart tremble. The rosary in her hand caught the sunlight beaming through the parlor window and sparked it into her eyes.

"You're nice to say that. And I'm sorry about your wife. My mom died last week. Her old dog needs a home, and my brother is my last hope. I guess I'll have to e-mail him. But I wanted to talk to him." Her voice shook, and Lily bit her lip hard to avoid making a blubbering fool of herself. Not that it mattered, she thought. She was talking to a stranger she'd never talk to again.

"I'm sorry about your mom," he said.

"It was a stroke," she replied.

"My wife was in the World Trade Center."

Rosa

"Oh!" Goosebumps pricked Lily's arms. "I am so sorry. My divorce was final few days before 9/11. I was spending that week with my mom. We sat that whole day together on the sofa watching it on TV. I am so sorry, Travis."

Looking down at the rosary, Lily remembered her mother praying the rosary while they watched the Twin Towers melt again and again, her mother's fingers slowly moving over the same beads Lily now cradled in her palm. Lily remembered feeling strangely angry with her mom, wanting to yank the beads away.

She'd asked her mom, "What good does that do?"

"It helps me," her mom had replied.

So Lily had joined in for a few Hail Marys, but reciting the prayers did nothing for her, and so she'd fallen silent and turned up the sound on the TV.

Now Lily could hear Travis breathing. "Thank you," he said. "After the first tower fell, I stopped watching. And I haven't watched any of the footage since. I can't. I feel like I'm watching her murder. But it comforts me—maybe this makes me seem weird—but it comforts me to know that the world was watching. She wasn't alone."

"It doesn't make you seem weird, Travis. Thank you for sharing that with me."

"Say," he said. Now his voice was louder, cheerful. "Tell me about your dog."

Lily began to talk. She slipped the rosary back into her pocket. She moved next to Rosa and stroked her back as she told Travis how, a few weeks after 9/11, her mother adopted Rosa from a shelter. She told how Rosa was a rambunctious golden retriever/possibly collie mix who'd mellowed into a well-mannered, affectionate dog. She told how Rosa loved to please, take leisurely walks, doze in sunbeams, and have her back scratched.

Travis laughed. "I like the same things!" He paused. The line crackled, like rain against glass. Lily gripped the phone so hard her hand cramped. Had the call dropped?

But then he started speaking, so quietly she held her breath.

"I don't know your name," he said.

"Lily. I'm Lily."

"Lily," he said. "Easter Lily."

"Easter Lily," she repeated.

"Easter Lily, I could be in Illinois on Tuesday. Could I meet Rosa? If we like each other, maybe she could be my traveling buddy. My son will be leaving me when we get to his new job tomorrow. It'll just be me and the open road. I think a friend like Rosa is just what I need."

•

TUESDAY MORNING, LILY took Rosa to a dog groomer for a bath and a brush. She took herself to a salon for a French braid and a manicure. Back in her mother's home, she sat in the kitchen with Rosa at her feet and watched the minutes tick on the clock over the refrigerator. Her stomach churned the way it had when she'd waited for her brother to show up at her wedding. It churned the way it had when she'd waited for her husband to come home late from work, smelling of another woman's perfume. It churned the way it had when she was a little girl, listening to her mother cry in the bathroom because Lily's father had stopped showing up.

Travis had said he'd arrive around noon. It was noon.

"Am I an idiot?" she asked Rosa.

Rosa just blinked her eyes.

But at 12:20 a motor home rumbled up the street and filled her mother's driveway. She thrust her hand into her sweater pocket and squeezed the rosary. "Hail Mary, Our Father, and Glory Be," she murmured. The butterflies squabbling in her stomach settled down.

She opened the front door.

He was tall and slim. His hair was white and thick, and his beard was gray and neatly trimmed. His blue eyes matched the color of his faded jeans.

He held a bouquet of lilies and a plate of cookies.

"Thank you!" Lily said. She reached for the cookies. Behind her, Rosa's tail thumped rapidly against her legs.

"The cookies are for Rosa," Travis said. "I baked them from a recipe I got online after we talked. The secret ingredient is chopped dried chicken liver."

Lily laughed. "They look great!"

•

IN THE MOTOR home, Rosa sniffed everything and soon settled herself on the couch.

They sat on each side of Rosa. Travis scratched Rosa's back. Rosa rested her head in his lap.

"Do you think I've made a new friend?" Travis asked.

"Two friends," Lily heard herself say. She felt a blush heat her face.

Travis went very still. Only his fingers moved, stroking Rosa's back.

"Are you free for dinner tonight?" he asked. "I make a mean Chicken Cordon Bleu. No chopped chicken liver, I promise."

Lily laughed. "Dinner would be nice."

She rubbed Rosa's left ear. Travis rubbed Rosa's right ear. Their fingers met.

Rosa began making soft, throaty rumbles.

"That's her rosary sound," Lily explained. She gave the backstory to Travis. He laughed and pulled a black-beaded rosary from a pocket on his jeans.

"Shall we join her?" he asked.

•

DURING THE THIRD decade, Lily watched something wonderful happen. Rosa's eyes began to drift shut. They'd snap open, then drift closed.

You're safe, sweetheart, Lily thought as she and Travis prayed. *Let yourself enjoy a nap. We'll both be here when you wake up.*

By the fourth decade, Rosa was fast asleep.

Scaredy Cat
First published in *Downstate Story* (2016)

"INSULIN SHOTS? YOU mean with a needle?"

The vet smiled. "It's not hard, Nick. I'll show you."

Nick watched the vet draw insulin from a vial into a syringe, then lift Taco's skin at the scruff. The vet inserted the needle.

Nick felt blood drain from his face. His legs shook.

"There!" the vet said. "All done!"

Taco purred and gobbled a treat from the vet's hand.

"Brave boy," the vet said.

Nick shook his head. "I'm not brave when it comes to needles."

The vet laughed. "I was talking to your cat, Nick. Don't worry. You'll do fine."

The vet gave Nick more instructions, then sent him on his way.

When Nick reached his apartment building—a six-unit brick building two blocks north of Wrigley Field—he saw that once again his neighbor's visiting fiancé had parked his Lexus in Nick's assigned spot. Street parking was nonexistent on game days at Wrigley, but today the Cubs were playing out of town. Street parking was still a challenge, but not impossible.

Taco was meowing, anxious to leave the cat carrier in the back seat. The building's remaining five parking spots had cars. Nick grabbed his cell phone and called his neighbor.

"Hey, Nick," Kate answered.

"Brad's car is in my spot," Nick said. "Again."

"It is? Oh, Nick, I'm sorry. He'll be right out to move it."

Minutes passed. Finally, both Kate and Brad appeared, Kate apologizing, Brad scowling. Nick lowered his car window, scowled back at Brad, and shook his head.

"Why are you still using my parking space, Brad? I thought you agreed to stop doing that."

"Chill, dude," Brad said. "Street parking's bad around here."

"Right," Nick replied. "That's why I need *my* spot so I can park and get my unhappy cat inside."

"Taco sure is crying," Kate said. "Everything OK?"

"Vet just diagnosed him with diabetes. I'll be giving him insulin shots twice a day!"

"It's a *cat*," Brad said. "Just replace it with a healthy one. Or better yet, get a dog. Cats are for little girls and grandmas."

"Brad!" Kate punched his arm. "Loving in sickness and health applies to pets, too!"

Brad laughed and patted Kate's head. "No worries, Kitten. You're too cute to replace."

Nick rolled his eyes and wondered again what his pretty neighbor saw in Brad. Sure, Brad was a handsome lawyer in a huge Chicago firm where Kate worked as a paralegal. One year ago, Brad had won a nice jury award for Kate's grandpa who'd suffered severe whiplash and broken ribs when a CTA bus rear-ended his Ford Focus. Kate's grandpa had slammed on his brakes to avoid hitting a dog who'd run into the street. The CTA had unsuccessfully argued contributory negligence. So, of course Kate's whole family was probably forever grateful for Brad's personal injury litigation chops. Nick figured that Brad probably earned triple Nick's salary as a public grade school teacher one year from tenure.

But still!

Brad drove off to find parking, and Kate accompanied Nick to his apartment. Nick opened the cat carrier, and Taco shot out to his favorite spot on the sofa.

"Taco can move pretty fast for an old boy!" Kate exclaimed. She sat on the sofa next to Taco and rubbed his ears. Taco began to purr. Kate knew the story: how Nick and his wife had adopted Taco from a shelter, and when they divorced, Nick kept Taco because his ex's new boyfriend was allergic to cats. Nick had told Kate the whole story during one of their occasional runs together along the lakefront.

Now Taco climbed into Kate's lap and closed his eyes.

"So," Kate said. "Insulin shots?"

Nick sighed. "I hate needles. I'll just have to get over it."

"Are you saying," Kate asked, "that you're a scaredy cat when it comes to needles?"

Nick felt his face grow warm. "I guess I am. Don't tell my sixth graders that!"

"Aww," Kate said. "Everyone's a scaredy cat about something."

"What frightens you?"

She looked at the diamond ring on her finger. Her dark eyebrows pinched into a slight frown. She bit her lower lip. The only sound was Taco's purring.

She's scared of the next step, Nick thought. *Brad's not the right guy for her! Come on, Kate! Just say it! You are way too good for him!*

"I'm scared," Kate said, "of spiders."

Nick forced a smile. "I saw Taco eat one once."

Kate laughed. "My hero!" She gently moved Taco off her lap and stood. "Brad should be back soon from his search for a parking spot. I better get back to the meatballs baking in my oven. Spaghetti and meatballs and bruschetta. Brad's special request for dinner. We're celebrating the one year anniversary of our first date."

Nick nodded. He could not bring himself to say congratulations. He knew it was also the one year anniversary of the jury award for Kate's grandpa. Brad and Kate's family had gone out after court for a celebratory lunch. Brad had just happened to have two tickets to an evening performance at The Lyric Opera House. How could Kate say no?

She'd later confessed to Nick that she didn't like opera, but Brad was determined to turn her ears into opera ears.

Nick knew that Brad had also given her a year's subscription to the Lyric for her last birthday, though Kate had hinted that she'd wanted tickets for Carrie Underwood at Ravinia.

Nick—though he did like opera—would have bought her the country music tickets. People should get what they want, Nick believed, not what others want them to want.

"Hey!" The dimples in Kate's smile hit Nick square in the heart. "Show me what to do, Nick. I'll give Taco his shots! I owe you for Brad always taking your parking spot when he visits."

•

THEY SOON SETTLED into an easy routine. Mornings before work they'd have coffee in Nick's kitchen, and Kate would give Taco his first shot. Evenings, Kate always managed to fit Taco in, even when Brad-outings loomed. If neither Kate nor Nick had other plans, they would have a glass of wine over a Scrabble game, then Kate would give Taco the second shot. When Kate was around, Taco acted as playful as a kitten. One time, Taco knocked a Scrabble tile to the floor and batted it around like a hockey puck. Soon, Kate and Nick found themselves laughing and kicking at the Scrabble tile, too.

Then one morning Kate showed up with puffy eyes. She slumped on Nick's sofa. Taco jumped in her lap, and she stroked his fur. Nick sat next to her. He kept his eyes on Kate's hand trembling in Taco's fur. The diamond in her engagement ring caught the sunlight shining through the window behind the sofa.

Damn sun, Nick thought.

"I have to do something really hard," she said.

"Oh?" Nick felt his heart jolt.

"We've set a date," she said. "Nick, I've been meaning to tell you, but..."

"Oh?" Nick forced a smile. "That's great!" *How*, he wondered, *could a smile hurt so much?*

"My lease is up next month. No point in renewing it, Brad says. He wants me to move into his condo."

"That makes sense," Nick said. "I mean, you've set a date..." His voice trailed off. He clenched his hands. So, he told himself, the hard thing she had to do was tell him she wouldn't be coming by anymore. Maybe she was even starting to sense that their time together was (pathetically?) the best part of his day. So, even though he and Kate weren't a couple, she was going to be breaking up with him like they were a couple. It was going to hurt like they were a couple. Well, he'd try to get through this with at least some dignity intact.

"Hey!" he said, his voice so loud and cheerful he saw her flinch. "I've watched you give Taco his shots enough times that I can do it no problem. Starting right now! You can go! Thank you! Thank you for helping me get over my fear of needles!"

He stood. "So, hey. I'll be fine. I'll walk you to the door!"

"Nick!" She looked up at him. "I have to do this. I'm the one being the scaredy cat now, but I have to do it. I . . ."

Nick lifted his hands. "It's OK. You don't have to spell it out for me. I get it. You can go. No hard feelings. Really."

Two pink spots flared in her cheeks. "Not yet."

Nick felt his own face heat up. "You're getting married," he said.

"We set a date," she said.

Nick felt something pop in his chest. The last tiny kernel of hope.

"My best friend wants to start shopping for bridesmaid dresses. My mom e-mailed me a list of caterers. My dad told me that Brad can start calling him *Dad*. It's all good, right? Brad is great in so many ways. He's generous, hardworking, handsome as hell, but"—she rubbed the wetness under her eyes—"hey, he would've replaced Taco in a heartbeat!"

"No one's perfect," Nick murmured.

She nodded. "No one's perfect."

"So what's the problem, Kate?"

"Brad," she whispered, "isn't you."

Nick stared at her. Then he sat back down on the sofa. Next to her. So close he could smell a strawberry scent in her hair. He loved strawberries.

She took a deep breath. She looked for a long moment at her engagement ring. Suddenly, she twisted it off and set it on the coffee table.

Taco jumped after it. With a swipe of his paw, he batted the ring under the couch.

Sincerely, Emma
First published as "A Letter from Emma" in *Storyteller* (2006)

EVERYTHING SHE WANTED was in the U-Haul. She was leaving behind the kitchen table and chairs, king-sized water bed, red leather sofa, and the floor-to-ceiling shelves Rashid had built.

A pad of paper was on the table, but no pen.

From her purse to the table she spilled out Kleenex, lip balm, aspirin, eye drops, a mouth guard, keys, wallet, phone, unredeemed winning instant lottery tickets, her hand-held electronic poker game, her Kindle.

No pen.

She looked at the boxes and bags piled on the living room floor. They were filled with stuff she didn't need or want.

God knows, she thought, *which box has pens*. She looked out the window at the cloudless blue sky. "Or if you do know, God," she said, "you're not about to enlighten me. You're kinda predictable that way."

She ran out to the U-Haul but found neither pen nor pencil in the glove compartment.

Back in the kitchen she opened empty cabinet drawers. In one drawer, what had been the catch-all drawer, a rather handsome red fountain pen rolled to the front.

"Well, thank you, God." She raised her fist toward the ceiling. "I owe you one."

She shook the pen, heard ink sloshing inside the barrel. She couldn't recall ever seeing the pen before. Probably it had been Rashid's. He'd gravitated to the old-fashioned. When they'd divorced, all he'd taken from their apartment besides his clothes and books had been the rotary phone, his Sears one-speed bike, and the tube radio that got only AM stations.

Well, it was her good luck that he'd left behind his little retro fountain pen.

She carried the pen to the table and sat before the pad of paper—yellow, lined, legal-sized. For a long time, she held the pen motionless above the paper.

Late afternoon sun knifed through the Levelor-blinded windows. The pen's nib caught the sun, firing light into her eyes, reminding her of how, during long meetings at work, she'd fire into her eyes the fluorescent light caught by her diamond ring.

The ring was back with Rashid. It had been his grandmother's. Now his second wife was probably wearing it.

The room darkened. She lowered her head and began to write.

Hello, Family, or more accurately, Goodbye Family.

You won't see me again. I'm going away because I want to become myself, and I can't do that when you already think you know who I am. Or should be. Your idea of me is a Halloween costume glued to my skin. I'm sweating and itching inside that costume.

So, I'm ripping it off.

And if I lose some skin in the process, well, skin grows back.

Dear sister Anne, I'm not your "Divorced-Sister-Emma." I am your sister. I am divorced. But I am not your "Divorced-Sister-Emma."

And tell your son and daughter that I am not their "Funny-Auntie-Emmy" who looks forward to babysitting them, who loves them like they're her own, because "Poor-Auntie-Emmy" doesn't have any children of her own, so it's really a favor to her when we have her babysit when Mommy and Daddy fly off to Maui, Paris, SF, Vegas, NYC, Ad Nauseum.

And guess what, Anne? I don't forgive your little Derek. I will never forgive him for what he did to my cat. I have this recurring dream. I'm slicing rosy red apples and flinging the rosy red slices to the bottom of the pool outside my apartment building.

Do you see the symbolism?

Need a hint?

Just take a look at your son's rosy red apple cheeks.

Emma put down the pen and closed her eyes. Again she saw a white blob shimmering under five feet of sparkling, chlorine-scented water. She saw herself patting Derek's rosy apple cheeks. She heard him sobbing, "It was so hot, Auntie Emmy. I was trying to cool Taco off, teach him to swim."

She remembered her father standing across the pool from her, and when she met his somber gaze, she smiled. It was a joke! One of her dad's practical jokes! That wasn't her fat white cat at the bottom of the pool. It was just a stuffed animal Dad had tossed down there. Dad was famous for his jokes. Practical jokes were his hobby. And today, his birthday, with all the family at her apartment for his party, he was treating himself to a practical joke at her expense.

By the time she understood the truth, it was too late. She was already patting the blubbering boy on his rosy red apple cheeks and telling him it wasn't the end of the world. It was just a cat.

Except it wasn't.

Emma picked up the pen.

Dear Mom,

I know I'm your Big Disappointment. Sturdy. That's how you consoled me when my size kept me from running round-off flip-flops in your gymnastics footsteps.

And Dad,

I'm sorry about not being tough enough to continue the U of C tradition. I'm sorry I dropped out of one of the country's top law schools. I'm sorry I sat on the bench on my high school softball team.

I'm sorry I looked like a softball player but played like a tub.

Yep. I overheard you describe me that way.

And I'm sorry I stayed home reading Stephen King ("Carrie," hah!) the night of my senior prom. How you cried, Mom. "Will she ever find someone?" you asked Dad.

Oops. Then came Rashid.

I didn't get a law degree from the University of Chicago, but I sure found a husband there.

Except he wasn't the right religion. His nose was too big and his ancestors were too exotic. He didn't want children. He didn't want a house in the suburbs.

He was perfect, I was sure.

But when my marriage ended, when Rashid said to me—"Emmy, it's not that I don't love you anymore. It's that I love someone else more."—I realized something.

My broken marriage wasn't just my failure.

It was also your success.

Rashid was the opposite of what you wanted in a son-in-law. Just like I know I'm the opposite of what you wanted in a daughter.

But parents can't divorce their kids, can they. So really, it's a favor to you, my gift to you, me disappearing out of the family like this.

And Anne, now you won't have to worry about your Derek's rosy red apple cheeks being sliced off by his poor crazed Auntie Emmy, even if it's just symbolically in my dreams.

I can hear you all now. Why is she writing all this? Why didn't she just talk to us?

You know why? Because we don't talk the same language. You want me to talk sunshine and flowers and achievements, but I've never learned that language.

I'm too sturdy, I guess.

Last month, a few days after Derek "accidentally" drowned Taco in the pool, I saw Rashid. I was stopped at a light, driving home from work. He was riding his bike.

And the guy who didn't want kids—well, my kids, I guess, kids who might have my dusty blonde hair and pasty pink skin—anyway, there was a coppery little kid bundled into a seat on the back of Rashid's bike. Toddler-sized. Rashid's wife was riding a bike behind him. Her hair was in long braids black as his.

"Ray-Ray!" she shouted. (My nickname for him.) "Slow down, cowboy!"

Again, Emma set down the pen. Again, she closed her eyes and waited for the lump in her throat to ease before continuing to write.

It's dark now. I can barely see what I'm writing.

I've quit my job, paid all my bills, shut off the utilities. I've got two months left on my lease. I'm letting the security deposit take care of that.

I'm off. To somewhere warm. Maybe near water. Maybe in a desert. I've developed a new hobby that I might indulge in if I head out west.

Don't worry. Divide the spoils as you will.

Oh, I plan to get another cat. But don't worry. I won't sign its name on your birthday and holiday cards. Because I won't be sending you any.

Sincerely, Emma.

Emma straightened her shoulders, set the pen down. Her heart raced. Sweat slicked her skin. She felt like she was sitting at a poker table with pocket aces, waiting for the flop.

It was a great feeling.

•

TWO WEEKS LATER, Emma's parents, worried because she wasn't returning their calls and texts, called her at work.

"She quit over a month ago," her boss said.

Emma's parents rushed to her apartment building and found the spare key still taped underneath the Weber grill on her rear deck. They let themselves into her unit. There they saw bags and boxes stacked along living room walls. They saw empty closets and drawers. Her mother ran from room to room, flinging open doors and crying out Emma's name.

In the kitchen, her father riffled through a yellow legal pad on the table, hoping to find a note of explanation. He lifted a red fountain pen next to the paper. It looked familiar.

On its metal clip, he read *Izzy Rizzy*.

Ah, he thought, *the trick shop.* He'd wondered what had happened to the pen. What fun he'd had with it a few years ago on April Fool's Day, writing out huge bonus checks for his paralegals and secretaries.

He'd gotten a little worried though. It had taken over an hour for the ink to disappear.

He pocketed the pen and went to comfort his wife, whom he could hear sobbing in the bedroom.

Slaughtering the Fatted Calf
First published in *St. Anthony Messenger* (2016)

GLORIA STUMBLED TOWARD the phone ringing on the kitchen wall.

No good news came right before dawn.

"Please, God," she prayed.

Had her daughter snuck out? Was Marin crying at the police station again, smelling of pot and beer?

Since that frightening episode last month, her daughter had been grounded, and Gloria had spent weekend nights in the family room dozing in the TV's glow, closer to the doors than she'd be upstairs where Charlie, her husband, snored softly.

Marin was 15, defiant and contemptuous. The sweet girl she'd once been had disappeared.

Gloria made the Sign of the Cross and answered the phone.

"Honey?"

"Dad!" *This* was the call she'd both dreaded and desired. "Is Mom . . . ?"

"Glory, I woke you, didn't I. But your mom wanted you to know right away. We're on speaker phone. Viv, tell Glory the wonderful news!"

Her mother shouted, "My Lorna's coming home!"

Lorna? Gloria's knees wobbled. Her sister had avoided the family for four years, ever since their mother was diagnosed with Alzheimer's, leaving all the caregiving to Gloria and their father, who was confronting early Parkinson's.

"Lorna's coming for Easter!" her mother yelled.

"Dad, it's three a.m. Did Lorna just call you?"

"It's not three a.m. in Singapore."

"She's in Singapore?"

"We'll have a party!" her mother shouted. "We'll invite everyone! I want lamb cakes and beef tenderloin!"

Beef tenderloin? Beef tenderloin was over $200 at the butcher. Gloria had been planning on ham for their Easter meal.

"She's arriving the Wednesday before Easter," her dad said. "Can you pick her up from the airport, Glory?"

Her mother was talking now, but Gloria wasn't listening. She was remembering her last phone call to Lorna four years ago. Her sister, living in Seattle, had just gotten divorced.

"What's up?" Lorna had asked. "I'm on the clock. Got a plane to catch for my Switzerland ski trip."

Gloria explained their mother's terrifying diagnosis.

"This should be a wake-up call for both of us," Lorna said. "What a legacy our parents are sticking on us, Dad's Parkinson's or Mom's dementia. At least you've got a daughter and husband to take care of you, if the time comes. Who's going to help me? I'm not going to waste a second of my health. And you shouldn't either."

"The job now, Lorna, is to care for Mom. We'll have to work as a team. You, Dad, me."

"There's not much I can do from Seattle," Lorna said. "My job's here. And I'd never move back to Chicago. How anyone can live without mountains and ocean—"

"It's not about you now, Lorna! God, you're self-absorbed. No wonder your husband dumped you. I'm surprised it took him so long."

Silence. Gloria heard a soft click. Not even a goodbye.

Now, four years later, just before a Sunday dawn, Lorna had announced her return.

•

LATER THAT MORNING, Gloria sat between her husband and daughter in their usual pew. During the homily, Marin began texting on her phone.

Gloria was too disturbed by the homily to grab the phone away.

"So remember," Father Gallagher was saying from the pulpit, "there is more joy in Heaven over the one who strays and then returns than over the 99 who need no salvation."

Gloria sighed. What a thundering coincidence, hearing this right at the beginning of her own prodigal sibling drama.

In the car after Mass, only Charlie made an effort to talk. From the back seat came the soft clicks of Marin texting. Gloria sighed.

"Who're you mad at now, Mother?" Marin sighed loudly, imitating Gloria.

"Your mom doesn't like Luke's Gospel of the Prodigal Son," Charlie said. "Especially now with your prodigal Aunt Lorna coming for Easter."

"So what's the prob, Mother? You're always complaining how Auntie Lorna doesn't help with Grandma. You should be happy she's coming. Just like that father in the gospel is happy his 'bad' son has come home."

Gloria turned toward her daughter. Marin was looking out the open car window, the wind blowing her overlong bangs from her overpainted eyes.

"I'll tell you what the *prob* is, Marin. I think the good son is getting a raw deal. The father slaughters the fatted calf and throws a big party to celebrate his bad son's return, but the hardworking good son has never even been given a young goat to feast on with his friends. Heck, he wasn't even told about the party! He returns from toiling in his father's fields and finds everyone feasting on the fatted calf! And then, what fries me the most, is when the father basically tells his good son that 'Hey, you're always around, and everything I have is yours anyway. So stop whining.' Like the good son is out of line for wanting a little recognition and appreciation!"

Charlie laughed, though Gloria saw that he was white-knuckling the steering wheel. "Gloria," he murmured. "I don't think that's quite what the father said."

"No, but he implied it! Anyway, don't you agree that Heaven's got it backwards? There should be more joy in heaven for the good sons, not the bad ones who live it up and then, only when they hit rock bottom, 'return to the fold.'"

Gloria looked at her daughter. "Your thoughts, Marin?"

Marin rolled her eyes. "Lighten up, lady. It's just a stupid story." Her phone warbled and she lifted it.

"Put that down!" Gloria snapped. "And apologize for calling me lady!"

"What? Seriously? I don't think so!"

"I'm waiting!" Gloria yelled.

"Ladies!" Charlie exclaimed.

"Fine," Marin said. "Sorry." She put down her phone and resumed looking out the window.

They finished the drive home in silence.

•

ON THE WEDNESDAY before Easter, it was just Lorna and Gloria on the 40-minute drive from the airport to their parents' home. Charlie was working, Marin at school. Navigating through heavy traffic, Gloria listened while Lorna answered calls on her phone.

"Sorry," Lorna said between calls. "I'm leading a hike up Mt. Rainier when I get back to Seattle, and there's a bunch of details to work out."

"Aren't you the busy little gal," Gloria said.

Lorna thrust her phone into her purse. "What's with the *baditude*, Gloria? I'm giving up seven vacation days to be here. I'm giving up being with people who love me, and who I love, to spend time with this family. This *biological* family of mine. Not the family of my heart."

"You've ignored your *biological* family for four years, Lorna. Hearts need blood flow to keep beating. You haven't *flowed* so much as a Christmas card to your *biological* family for four years."

"Mom and Dad sure seemed happy to hear from me. You should hear what Mom had to say about you. She called you bossy, crabby. Said toads and spiders fall out of your mouth whenever you open it. She actually said that, Gloria."

Gloria's heart churned. "Let's see what she says about you after the next week. You wanna fill in for me? Change her diapers, cajole her into the tub, fix diabetic-safe meals, trick her into taking her meds, drive her to three different doctors?"

"Christ, Gloria! Your husband supports you. Your daughter is old enough to take care of herself. What else you gotta do?"

They didn't speak again until Gloria parked in front of their parents' home. "Have fun," Gloria said.

"You're not coming in?" Lorna asked. Gloria heard the panic in her sister's voice. She kept her eyes on the steering wheel and shook her head.

Suddenly, Lorna laughed. "Oh my Lord! No way!"

Gloria looked up. Gasped. There, bouncing down the front steps, was Marin.

Lorna shot from the car. "Look at you, girl! All grown-up! A gorgeous young woman!"

Marin hugged Lorna. Gloria frowned. When was the last time she'd gotten hugged by her daughter? She stumbled from the car.

"Marin! What are you doing here?"

Marin stepped out of Lorna's embrace. "Dad left work early, picked me up from school. We're here to welcome Auntie Lorna."

Charlie appeared in the front door, flanked by Gloria's parents, all three of them smiling and waving.

At Lorna.

Traitors, Gloria thought.

•

THEY HAD PIZZA delivered. While they ate, Lorna chattered about her trips, job, and friends.

"It's getting late," Charlie finally said. "I'll take Marin home. School night for her. Work for me."

Gloria stood, too.

"You can stay, honey," Charlie said. "Maybe catch Lorna up with *our* life."

Gloria shook her head and sighed.

"Lorna!" their mother shouted. "You don't have to leave too, do you? You still have to tell us what's new with you."

That's all we've been hearing, Gloria thought.

"Viv," Gloria's dad said. "Lorna's not leaving. She's staying right here with us for a whole week! For Easter!"

"Oh!" Gloria's mother clapped her hands. "Let's have a party!"

Lorna laughed. "You know, Mom, if you had a computer, I could Skype and e-mail you all the time, send you photos of my adventures and friends."

Lorna frowned at Gloria. "I'm surprised you haven't set them up with a computer yet, Gloria."

"Oh, That One," their mother said, scowling at Gloria. "I don't want to bother That Lazy One with stuff like that."

Gloria felt tears well.

"Now, Viv." Gloria's dad patted his wife's head. "Our Glory does a lot for us. We'd be lost without her."

I won't cry, Gloria thought even as her tears began to spill. Suddenly, Marin flung her arm over Gloria's shoulders and pulled her close.

"No school Friday for me, Auntie Lorna," Marin said. "How about you and me go shopping for a computer then? I could help you pick one out for Grandma and Grandpa. We could have it up and running before Mom makes me go to Good Friday services."

"That's a great idea, Marin," Charlie said. "And Lorna, this'd be a good way for you to cover all those Christmases and birthdays you've missed."

Gloria smiled at the shock blanching her sister's face.

"I think I *will* stay for a bit," Gloria said.

As soon as Charlie and Marin left, Lorna whispered to Gloria. "Let's take a walk. We have to talk."

•

FOR THE FIRST block, they walked in silence. "Look, Gloria," Lorna finally said. "I can't afford to buy them a computer. My job is shaky. I may not survive the next reorganization. My townhouse is worth less than my mortgage. I'd like to get Lasik surgery this year, but it's not covered by my insurance."

"So this is why you've come home? To hit our parents up for money?"

"You don't get it, Gloria. You've got it all. A husband who loves and supports you. A great daughter."

Gloria shook her head. "Marin's not always so great to me. I've been so busy mothering our mother that I've neglected mothering my own daughter. My loving little girl has disappeared. We argue constantly. Her grades could be better. Her mouth could be way better."

"When you were helping Mom in the bathroom before the pizza came," Lorna said, "Marin told me how awesome you were with the police when she had that bit of trouble."

"She said that?" Gloria felt her face warm. "Though I wouldn't call getting busted for underage drinking and pot a *bit* of trouble."

Lorna sighed. "Marin's a good girl. But she's not you. So she partied a little bit. I did that too around her age. She wants your acceptance, warts and all. That's what's killing her, Gloria. She thinks you don't think she's good enough."

"You've seen her for a few hours today and you somehow know all that? You have no standing, Lorna, to be telling me anything about my daughter."

Lorna sighed again. "Well, you've done a great job taking care of Mom, helping Dad. He told me that."

"So now you're buttering me up, Lorna? Planning to ask *me* for your Lasik money?"

Lorna groaned. Then she spun around and strode back toward the house.

Gloria froze. She felt her stomach twist, her heart pound. Something thick and sticky filled her throat. She watched her sister move farther and farther away.

Like her mother.

Like her daughter.

The three women she loved most. Disappearing.

A cry exploded from her throat. "Wait! Lorna! Come back!" She ran after her sister, tripped, fell, and suddenly Lorna was there, helping her up, both of them crying.

"I'm sorry," Gloria said. "I'm doing it again. I drove you away four years ago with my mouth, and I'm doing it again."

Lorna wiped her own wet eyes. She hugged Gloria. "I *was* angry," Lorna murmured. "I *am* angry. You've said a lot of hurtful things to me. But I guess I've just been using my anger at you as an excuse to be uninvolved in Mom's care. Truth is, both of them falling apart like they are, it freaks me out. Scares me. I'm sorry I haven't been helping you, Gloria."

They stepped apart and sighed at the same time. Lorna started laughing, and after a moment, Gloria joined in.

•

HOLY SATURDAY NIGHT, Gloria woke suddenly. Had she heard the front door open and close? Charlie snored softly. She looked at the clock on her nightstand. Just after two.

Go back to sleep, Gloria scolded herself. She'd soon be busy. A big feast to prepare after church.

Marin is home sleeping, Gloria told herself. *She is.*

Hating the heaviness in her gut, Gloria sat up. She eased from bed and padded down the hall to Marin's room. The door was closed. Gloria pushed it open.

Marin's bed was empty.

Gloria leaned against the wall for a long time, staring at Marin's empty bed. Then she trudged to the stairs that would lead to the family room, where she would sit and wait for her daughter to return.

Downstairs she saw that light spilled from the kitchen. Voices murmured. Gloria stood in the dark dining room, gazing through the pass-through opening in the wall between the dining room and kitchen.

Seated at the kitchen table were Marin and Lorna. Marin was icing the lamb cake that Gloria had made yesterday. Lorna was wrestling the beef tenderloin, cursing softly as she trimmed it and tied it with string. Gloria could hear something bubbling on the stove. And now she realized that the dining room table had been set. Even the water goblets were out, ready to be filled.

Her eyes warmed.

She felt her lips bloom into a smile.

Tenley's Mouse
First published as "Tenley's Apology" in *Brain, Child* (2014)

MARY IS SEARCHING in the fridge for an unblemished apple for her daughter when she hears Tenley scream from upstairs.

Mary sighs, finds a perfect apple, and drops it into Tenley's lunch bag.

"Mother!" Tenley shouts. "Come here! Hurry!"

Mary looks at the clock on the microwave. Her hands clench into fists. In 30 minutes Tenley must leave for school. Already this morning, her 15-year-old daughter has had two crises. What new problem looms?

Menstrual cramps? A forgotten homework assignment absolutely due today? What problem might Tenley manufacture this time? If she misses one more day this semester, they'll have to get a doctor's note to confirm an illness. The school allows only seven parentally excused absences each semester.

•

EARLIER THIS MORNING, Tenley had complained of swollen eyelids.

"Hot or cold cloths on eyes?" she'd asked. Tenley, slim and beautiful in her tee shirt and shorts, was standing in front of the big mirror hanging in the hallway outside her bedroom.

Mary remembered how she and her husband had carefully carted the mirror home from T. J. Maxx, hung it, and then had fun in front of it. Sixteen years ago, when Mary was still young (36) and arrogantly confident, the mirror a witness to Tenley's beginning.

Mary stood next to her only child, gazed at their side-by-side reflections. She saw the wrinkles and graying hair that she usually didn't notice. The glow from Tenley's smooth young body created a brutal spotlight.

"I don't know what's better for swollen eyelids," Mary said, "but your eyelids look fine."

"They're not fine! Look at them! I can't go to school looking like this! I hardly slept again last night. I've got insomnia, but you don't care. I've been asking you and asking you to make a doctor's appointment. I can't sleep! I wake up tired! I need pills!"

"Your eyelids look fine," Mary insisted. "But I'll Google to find out if you should use hot or cold on them."

"And I need a private tutor for ACT prep like all my friends have!"

"You don't need a private tutor for the ACT. Have you even opened that book of practice tests I got you last month? Plus you're signed up for those after-school prep classes your school offers for free. That starts soon, next month I think."

"I have insomnia! You don't care!"

In the mirror, their reflections scowled at each other.

"Have you turned off your laptop and cell phone at night like your dad and I told you to? Are you texting or Facebooking when you should be sleeping?"

Tenley marched to the bathroom. Mary followed. Tenley slammed the door in Mary's face. "You don't know anything," Mary heard Tenley mutter. "What good are you."

And then, most awful, "Old lady, you are such a *beyotch*."

Mary sighed and returned to the kitchen to make a salami sandwich for Tenley's lunch. "Old lady," she murmured. "Nothing wrong with being a 52-year-old lady."

She resolved to battle if her daughter wanted to stay home from school today because of the imaginary swollen eyelids.

But the other battles could be postponed.

She opened a drawer at the kitchen desk, took out her to-do list. There were three items still active on it.

P-$, code for *pay bills*.

Sch Col. That item, *schedule colonoscopy*, had been on her list since her 50th birthday, two years ago.

Tenley's Mouse

Ph-M. She grabbed a pen and crossed that item off. She'd phoned her mother yesterday, left a message on her answering machine. That counted, Mary decided.

Underneath Ph-M, Mary wrote: Dwt, DoA, code for *Discuss w/Tenley, the dignity of aging.*

That would have to happen at a more peaceful moment. There was a lot Mary could tell her daughter about why aging was a gift, not a curse, a privilege not readily available to their ancestors. What was that poem by Wislawa Szymborska that Mary had memorized in college? Lines from the poem suddenly flowed from Mary like a song:

> Few of them made it to thirty.
> Old age was the privilege of rocks and trees . . .
> One had to hurry to get on with life. . .
> Wisdom couldn't wait for gray hair.

I'll have Tenley read that poem, Mary decided. *We'll read it aloud together, discuss it.*

Mary shook her head. *Yeah, right,* she thought. *Like that'll ever happen.* She scowled at her to-do list. Why, she wondered, were her only good conversations with Tenley the ones that took place in her imagination?

She added a final item to the list. GTA. *Get Tenley's Apology.* She resolved to make her daughter apologize for calling her a *beyotch.* But after school, not before. Best to avoid any more before-school drama.

•

"MOTHER!" TENLEY YELLS again. "I said come here! Where are you?"

Mary pours herself another cup of coffee, takes two sips, longingly eyes the two newspapers waiting for her on the kitchen table. Maybe, Mary decides, she'll just ignore this latest mom-shout. Maybe Tenley's cell phone will warble a text from a friend and that'll distract her daughter from whatever new problem has arisen.

"Muhhhhther!" A screech.

"Tenley!" Mary screams. "What's the problem!" She slams down her coffee mug, feels the strain on her throat. Screams had ripped her throat during labor 15 years ago. She'd had no voice for four days. Now, she wonders if they both lost out on important bonding because she couldn't murmur love or sing lullabies during Tenley's first days of life.

Mary bonds well with the children who swarm her at the library where she works as head of youth programs. They draw pictures for her, tell her long involved stories about squabbles with friends or triumphs on the soccer fields and sometimes heartbreakers about sick siblings or divorcing parents.

She'd said as much to Tenley during one of their fights, how the library kids like her, talk to her.

"Well," Tenley had replied, "they don't have to live with you."

•

TENLEY'S NEXT SHOUT has nothing to do with illness or angst.

"There's a dead mouse in my room!"

Mary smiles, relieved. Not a Tenley crisis. Just a mouse. A dead mouse Taco must have caught and killed.

Taco is their fat white cat who prefers Tenley over Mary, though it's Mary who feeds Taco every morning. It's Mary who tends to Taco before the coffee is brewed, before the newspapers are fetched from the curb, before the husband is kissed goodbye. It's Mary who kneels daily before the litter tray.

Taco has apparently caught a mouse, killed it, and deposited the prize in Tenley's room.

Somewhere Mary remembers learning that a cat considers it a sign of respect when it presents its kill to a human. Mary feels a bit resentful that Taco hasn't deposited the dead mouse in her own bedroom.

From the kitchen, Mary shouts, "Pick up the mouse and throw it out!"

From upstairs, Tenley shouts back, "Are you kidding me? You do it! It's too gross!"

"It's too gross for me, too!"

"You're the adult!"

Mary rolls her eyes, sighs. As she gathers plastic gloves, a plastic bag, and paper towels, she mumbles all the claims Tenley frequently makes about being all grown-up

"I'm almost 16! My curfew should be midnight!"

"Stop checking my grades on Edline. School is my business, not yours! I'm old enough to take care of school without you getting so involved. You and Dad are such obsessive helicopter parents!"

"You don't trust me!"

"I can wear what I want!"

"Why can't I see R-rated movies with my friends?"

"Everybody in high school drinks. *Everybody.* You and Dad are the only parents so weird about it. *That's* why I never have my friends over . . . As soon as I turn 18, I'm moving out!"

Mary trudges upstairs to Tenley's room.

Her daughter has fled the room. "Tenley?" Mary calls out.

From the bathroom, Tenley shouts back, "Tell me when it's gone!"

Mouse is supine on the carpet by the bed.

Thank you, Lord, Mary thinks. Thank you that mouse is not *on* the bed, not on the $300 white down-filled comforter from Macy's which Mary knows Tenley would no longer be able to use if it had been contaminated by dead mouse.

Four tiny legs spike from the mouse's body, as though it were trying to swim away from death. Its torn, chewed belly is a red lumpy mess, like Mary imagines her own belly must have looked after the unplanned C-section released her daughter into the world, which 13 hours of hard labor had failed to accomplish.

"Just get it out!" Mary had begged.

Wisely, mouse has closed its eyes to the mess, like Mary had closed her own eyes when the squalling, frightening, slimy creature was placed near her breast for that all-important few moments of bonding.

The mouse's whiskers, delicate white silk, droop gracefully. Its tail is curled into the shape of a question mark.

How did that squalling, frightening, slimy creature turn so quickly into a beautiful young girl?

How could such a beautiful young girl be so brutally contemptuous toward her parents, to the two people who love her most? And especially, toward her mother?

Except often, Mary understands because sometimes, Mary feels no love for her daughter, either. Fatigue when she was a baby, boredom when she was a toddler, and now, now when her daughter's a teen, Mary notices within herself a simmering soup of anger, bewilderment, frustration, impotence.

She'd been a surprise. Mary had not wanted children. Too risky. Bad genes. Both her parents were alcoholics. Her husband had reluctantly agreed they'd remain child-free.

But accidents happen. Especially when two people are young and in love and delighted by their vigorous reflections in their big new mirror.

Mary kneels in front of the mouse. "Sorry, little one," she whispers.

She holds her breath, grabs the mouse with a gloved hand, drops it light as nothing into the plastic bag. She hurries downstairs, outside, and throws the bag into the garbage bin by the garage.

Back in the kitchen, she squirts antibacterial soap on her hands and scrubs them under the hottest tap water she can tolerate.

She returns to Tenley's room and sprays carpet cleaner on the spot where the mouse had been, though nothing visible stains the beige carpet. The mouse was polite to keep its death fluids to itself.

Ten minutes later, back in the kitchen, Mary hears Tenley telling her friends, Hazel and Alesha, about the mouse. The three teenagers sit around the kitchen table, eating cereal. The girls walk together to school every morning.

"You picked it up?"

"*Mais non! C'était la mère qui a touché la souris!*" Tenley says in French.

Mary decides not to feel hurt that Tenley said "It was *the* mother who touched the mouse," instead of "It was *my* mother who touched the mouse."

All three girls take French. When Tenley was in fourth grade and still sought Mary's opinions, she told Mary she had a big problem. The grade school was offering foreign language instruction during lunch twice a week.

"Everyone wants to take Spanish," Tenley had said. "They'll have to do a lottery. I probably won't get into Spanish. I *need* to get into Spanish, Mama!"

"Well," Mary had replied. "I minored in French in college. French is cool because in upscale French restaurants you'll be able to impress everybody when you order in French. Plus, trips to Paris are so much better when you can speak the language."

Later, Mary was driving her fourth grade daughter and a minivan-full of Girl Scouts home from a meeting. Behind the wheel, Mary was invisible the way chauffeur-parents are. The girls talked freely. Tenley explained to her friends why she was signing up for lunchtime French instead of Spanish.

Mary's reasons had become Tenley's.

The next day, so many fourth graders signed up for lunchtime French, the school had to use a lottery to see who could get into the sessions. That was the first time Mary realized how much influence Tenley had over her peers. And how much influence Mary herself could wield.

Until she couldn't.

•

"TELL THEM, MOM," Tenley says. "Tell them about the mouse."

For several minutes, Mary has the three teens' attention as she describes the ordeal of the dead mouse.

She makes it funny, scary, gross.

The girls laugh and groan. "Bravo, Mama!" Tenley exclaims.

A warm glow heats Mary's belly.

For a few minutes, dead little mouse is making things right, is restoring the proper balance.

Daughter is loving child.

Mother is respected adult.

Mouse is martyr.

Taco appears, mewling.

"Taco!" Tenley shouts. "Come to us, Butcher Boy! My friends want to smell your mouse breath!"

The friends shriek their protests.

Taco ignores the teens. He stays by Mary. He rubs his fat white head against Mary's legs.

The friends head for the front door. Tenley doesn't follow them. She kneels and pets Taco, still rubbing himself against Mary's legs.

Tenley looks up at Mary. "What's for supper, Mama?"

Instead of saying baked tilapia, which is what Mary had planned and which she knows Tenley doesn't much like, Mary hears herself offering, "How about spaghetti and meatballs?"

"Bruschetta, too?" Tenley asks.

Mary hesitates. That'll mean a trip to the grocery store on her lunch hour to get the tomatoes, garlic, lemon, basil, bread.

Tenley says, "I can pick up the ingredients after school."

"Okay," Mary says. "Will you help me make it?"

Tenley stands. "Okay," she says. She heads to the front door where her friends are waiting.

"Have a good day," Mary shouts.

"Thanks, you too, Mom!" Tenley shouts back.

The girls leave. Mary goes to the kitchen desk, removes her to-do list. She looks at the last item. GTA. *Get Tenley's Apology.*

She crosses it off.

What Good Moms Do
First published in *Brain, Child* (2015)

GRIFF AND GANNON tiptoed to the sparkling Christmas tree in their dad's family room. Behind the tree, early morning darkness pressed against the floor-to-ceiling windows.

The boys crouched in front of the tree. Ganny reached for the largest present. It was wrapped in a pattern of Santa heads. Across the heads, someone had printed in black ink: *To Griffin and Gannon, Love from Dad, Francesca, and Baby Guinevere.*

"You can't open it yet," Griff said. He shivered. The size and shape of the present reminded him of his sister's coffin. She'd been born too early, on Christmas Day five years ago. Ganny, of course, wouldn't remember. He'd only been 2 years old.

Ganny frowned. "One present for us? Where's the stuff from Santa?"

Griff shrugged. Ten years old, he knew Santa was fake. But Ganny was only 7. Their dad should've put Santa gifts under the tree. He wondered if their dad was even home. He'd left for work right after their mother had dropped them off early yesterday morning, and he'd still been gone when they went to bed last night.

Behind them, the floor creaked. Ganny froze. "Santa! Is it Santa? I can't look!"

The boys turned around. But it wasn't Santa who filled the doorway to the family room.

"You're up early," Francesca said.

Their stepmother shuffled into the room. Her green eyes bulged out at them over a cup the size of a softball. A big white bow, lumpy as cauliflower, sprouted from her dirt-black hair.

Griff hated cauliflower.

"Good morning," he said. "Merry Christmas."

"Merry Christmas, Griffin." Francesca looked at Ganny. "Merry Christmas, Gannon."

"Back at ya," Ganny said.

Griff bit his tongue—a trick his mother had taught him—so he wouldn't laugh.

Francesca shook her head and sighed.

Griff watched her waddle to the rocking chair. She still looked fat, he thought, even though her baby had been born a long time ago, right after Halloween. He watched her sink heavily into the rocker and slurp from her cup.

Ganny laughed. "You got spit-up all over your mouth!"

Griff bit his tongue again. The foam from her drink coated her fat lips, and it did look like spit-up.

He let himself smile.

"Shush," Francesca said as Ganny continued to laugh. "You'll wake your sister. And your dad." She wiped her mouth on the sleeve of her robe and looked at the clock on the fireplace mantel.

"Thirty more minutes, and then it will be OK to wake Guinevere. Schedules are very important to babies. Not even Christmas should interfere. Your sister needs her sleep. Your dad, too."

"Half-sister," Ganny muttered, too quietly for Francesca to hear.

"Mmm," Francesca said, rocking and sipping. "This cappuccino is blissful, just blissful. You know, boys, it was my mommy who sent me the cappuccino machine for Christmas this year. She can't wait to meet your baby sister."

"You're too old to say mommy," Ganny said.

Francesca's face turned red.

"Ganny!" Griff pinched his brother's arm. They'd promised their mother that they'd be polite while they stayed at their dad's. "She's not too old at all!" Then, before he could stop himself, he blurted what he'd heard their mother say. "She's closer in age to me than she is to Dad!"

The red on Francesca's face spilled to her neck.

"Is your mommy coming today?" Griff asked. Asking questions, he knew, was a good way to distract grown-ups from getting mad.

"No! She's not!" Francesca's thick black eyebrows plunged practically to her nose. "And I said *mommy* because you boys are still at the *mommy* age. I was using a kid word because I'm talking to kids!"

She sipped her drink. Her face returned to its normal milky color. Goosebumps pricked Griff's arms. He didn't think she would yell again, but with grown-ups, it was hard to know. At least since his parents' divorce, the yelling had mostly stopped.

And he didn't really mind Francesca so much. He'd hated That Other One, the one his dad had almost married before Francesca. That One had been prettier than Francesca, but she'd almost killed Ganny. Ganny had been rushed to the hospital after eating the white powder he'd found in her purse.

"The little shit shouldn't have been digging in my purse!" That One had yelled.

"You don't bring *your* little shit into *my* house when *my* boys are here!" their dad had yelled back.

•

"MY MOTHER," FRANCESCA was saying, "volunteers with Global Samaritans, and she spends Christmas with poor families. She's been so busy helping the poor families in Guatemala that she hasn't had a chance to meet your sister yet."

"Half-sister," Ganny muttered, a little louder this time.

"Stop punching buttons, you idiot," Griff whispered.

Francesca sighed. "However, when I was your age, boys, my mother always spent Christmas with me. Because that's what good moms do."

Griff had nothing to say to that. Even Ganny stayed silent. A few days ago, their parents had argued about their mom working again on Christmas. Griff had listened on the extension. It had something to do with Grace. His dad had said the f-word, and his mom had cried.

"My mother," Francesca was saying, "helped me make most of those ornaments on the tree. When your sister's older, I'll teach her how to make ornaments like my mother taught me. And that window?" She pointed to a stained glass window over the couch. "My mother and I worked on that together when I was about your age, Griffin. We won first prize for it at our club's art fair. Your dad had it installed last month. It's what I wanted for Christmas, having it put up in our family room. I like looking at it when I rock your sister."

"It's very nice," Griff said, though he hadn't noticed the stained glass window until now.

"Where's the stuff Santa brung?" Ganny asked.

Francesca stopped rocking. She cleared her throat. "You're going to love what's in that big present under the tree. It came all the way from Italy! I looked through a lot of catalogs and websites before I found the perfect gift for you boys."

"But where's the stuff Santa brung?" Ganny asked.

Francesca looked at Griff. "Your dad said you boys knew."

Griff bit his lip. He was in fourth grade. Of course, *he* knew.

"Knew what?" Ganny asked.

Francesca coughed. "Well." She looked at Griff. Red splotched her cheeks like a rash.

"Santa's bringing stuff to our real house," Griff said. "Not here, because that wouldn't be fair to kids who only have one house."

"That's right!" Francesca smiled at Griff.

He looked away without smiling back.

"I wanna go home now!" Ganny shouted.

Francesca flinched and shushed.

"Mom's not even home, you idiot," Griff said. "She's working a double shift at the hospital, remember?"

"You're the idiot!" Ganny yelled.

"Boys! Stop!" Francesca pressed her hands over her palpitating heart. "No name calling! Doesn't your mother teach you better?"

She rubbed her left eye to calm the eyelid's twitching. Off saving the world, their mother was, big shot emergency room doctor, too busy to take care of business in her own backyard. Foisting her kids on Francesca, a new mother with a borderline colicky baby. Lily had sent nothing when Guinevere was born, not even a card. Nothing to acknowledge that her sons now had a sister. Of course

What Good Moms Do

it was sad that Lily's own daughter had been born too early. But really, Lily had pushed for a third child for the wrong reason: to try to heal an ailing marriage, is how Gary had once explained it to Francesca.

Francesca knew how dumb that was. Francesca hadn't been enough to save her parents' marriage. They'd divorced when she was 2 years old.

Francesca still had the note—in her jewelry box—that her mother had tucked into the gift she'd given Francesca for her 16th birthday: *Pregnancy may land a man, but a child won't keep him.*

The gift was a box of birth control pills.

It was a hard truth Francesca would impart to her own daughter when the time came. Good mothers told hard truths. And a good mother would have sent a gift for her sons' new baby sister. Francesca's mother had sent a $500 gift card from Nordstrom. It was in Francesca's jewelry box. She and her mother would shop Nordstrom together for baby clothes. Her mother had promised a visit in spring.

Francesca felt tears prick her eyes. Spring was so far away. She felt a surge of sympathy for her stepsons. Of course they wanted their mom.

"I wanna go home now!" Ganny yelled. He scrambled behind the tree.

"Get him out from there!" Francesca cried. The sympathy she'd been feeling exploded into irritation. "He'll tip the tree!"

Francesca gasped as Griff went after his brother. "Boys! Careful!"

Gary padded into the room, yawning and rubbing his bald head.

"Hey, what's all this splendid commotion?" he asked, just as the tree began to shudder. He rushed to steady it, and the boys tumbled out.

"Merry Christmas, boys!" Gary shouted.

"Shush!" Griff and Francesca warned simultaneously.

"Yeah, shush up, Dad!" Ganny shrieked.

From upstairs, the baby's cries exploded.

"Oh!" Francesca shivered. Tears welled.

Gary patted her shoulder. "Aw, Kitten," he said. "I'll go do the diaper and bottle business. You just relax. Get yourself another coffee."

Francesca looked at the clock on the mantel. "OK, but she's not due for a bottle for another 15 minutes. So could you just change her? And be sure to use the cloth diapers, OK?"

She looked at the boys. Gannon's nose was dripping, and his eyes were wet.

"Wipe your nose, Gannon," she said.

He ignored her, and looked at Gary. "Can I help you, Daddy?"

"No!" Francesca said. "Just stay put, boys."

"Wipe your nose, sport," Gary said. "Stay put, OK?"

"Please," Francesca said to the boys. "Wait. Until. We're. All. Ready."

•

BY THE TIME everyone was ready, the tree, though still lit, no longer sparkled. Sunlight blazed through the windows behind the tree, spotlighting dust motes which swirled like nervous bugs in the beams of light. The tree no longer looked magical, Francesca thought. Just desperate, like an old woman wearing too much makeup. Like she found herself looking every time she glanced in a mirror.

She felt worn out. Old. She *was* old. A quarter of a century.

Something icy filled her throat. Guinevere's little body, blessedly still for the moment, warmed her lap, but every other part of Francesca felt cold. She shivered. Was she getting sick?

"Smile, Kitten!" Gary was pointing the camera at her. She smiled.

•

GANNY PULLED THE big package from under the tree.

"It's heavy!" he exclaimed.

Griff tried to lift it. It *was* heavy! Excitement tickled his stomach.

The boys tore off the ribbons and wrapping.

They stared at the present: a black suitcase on wheels.

"Wipe off those frowns, guys, and open it up," Gary said. "I'm sure you'll love whatever's inside."

They unzipped the case, flipped back the top. Inside were two rows of shiny balls, red ones and blue ones, each about the size of a baseball, and one smaller white ball. The letters GGG were painted on each colored ball. Their last name was painted on the white ball.

Ganny tried to lift the hard clear plastic which covered the balls, but thick staples held it fast. "What the heck?" he said. The boys looked at their dad, who was scratching his head.

"It's a bocce ball set," Francesca said. "The three Gs on the colored balls are for Griffin, Gannon, and Guinevere. The small white ball is called the pallino."

"Thank you," Griff said. "It's very nice." He thought of Grace, his real baby sister. Even though she was dead, he decided the third G would be for Grace.

"Dad, can you get the plastic off?" Ganny asked.

"Oh, Gary," Francesca said. "I think we should leave that for when they get back to their own home. I'd hate for any of the balls to get misplaced here."

"But we got nothing to play with now!" Ganny shrieked.

"Well," Gary said. "Maybe we can—"

"Boys," Francesca interrupted. "This is an authentic set. Hand-polished in Italy. The balls are solid cherry, so they're not to be left out when you're not using them. You'll have fun playing with it in your yard this summer. Gary, maybe you can suggest to Lily that she get a little bocce court put in for them."

"I wanna play with it now!" Ganny whined.

Francesca shook her head. "It's an outside game. And you don't know the rules yet."

"Dad!" Ganny cried. "So what are we gonna do now?"

Gary shrugged. "It's an outside game, sport."

"And we gotta get ready for church anyway," Griff said.

Francesca smiled at Griff. He looked away without smiling back.

•

AFTER CHURCH, FRANCESCA served dinner. Miraculously, Guinevere slept. The boys pushed their eggplant lasagna around on their plates and ignored the peas.

"I want tacos," Ganny said.

Francesca frowned. "Well, in this house, we don't eat anything with eyes."

"Well, these peas look like *your* eyes." Ganny shoved a spoonful into his mouth. "Gross!" He spat the peas back on his plate.

Griff felt his stomach twist. He watched Francesca's hands clench into fists on either side of her plate. She looked at his dad.

"Gannon!" His dad shook his head. "That was rude, sport. Apologize to your stepmother."

Griff could tell Ganny was biting his tongue. *Please don't stick it out*, he thought.

"Sorry," Ganny mumbled. He coughed. "*Stepmother*."

Francesca's mouth trembled.

Griff shoved a chunk of the eggplant lasagna into his mouth and forced himself to swallow it. "Tastes great!" he exclaimed.

Francesca's wet eyes landed on him. A smile dented her face.

He looked down at his plate.

For a moment, no one spoke.

"I've got rounds to make pretty soon," their dad said. "And the surgical res asked if I could cover for him because of some family emergency."

Francesca sighed. "I should probably nap while Guinevere is down." Again her wet green eyes landed on Griff.

"We can just watch TV 'til Mom comes to get us," Griff said.

•

AFTER THEIR DAD left for the hospital, Griff packed his and Ganny's duffel bags and put them by the front door. Francesca wheeled the bocce set next to their bags.

"OK, guys. The TV is all yours. Just keep the door to the family room closed so the TV won't wake your sister. And keep the sound low, OK?"

"Half-sister," Ganny muttered.

What Good Moms Do

Francesca handed a cell phone to Griff. "Your dad asked your mom to call when she gets here. I don't want her ringing the doorbell and waking me or your sister."

"Half-sister," Ganny said loudly, but Francesca had already left the room.

•

THEY WATCHED A *Sponge Bob* cartoon for a while. They sat on the floor close to the TV. At home, they each had a bean bag chair for watching TV. Their dad had promised he'd have bean bag chairs for them here, too. But there were no bean bag chairs.

"I'm bored," Ganny said. He went to the front door and wheeled the bocce set back into the family room. He took a fork from the dining room hutch and used it to pry off the staples, bending one of the prongs.

Griff slid the ruined fork under the couch.

For a while, they rolled the balls around the room.

"This is boring," Ganny said.

They began pitching balls to each other.

A red ball slammed into photos on top of the piano. Wedding photos toppled into baby photos. A wild pitch just missed the TV screen.

Ganny raced to field a high pop up. He crashed into an end table. A lamp fell.

Griff zoomed for a line drive. He tripped over the rocking chair and fell into the tree. The tree shuddered and tipped. Ornaments shattered. They propped the tree against the glass wall.

Griff jumped on the couch to catch a high fly ball just as the cell phone in his pocket rang. Distracted, he missed the ball. It slammed into the stained glass window over the couch. He heard a crack.

"Hi Mom," Griff said into the phone. "We're ready. We just have to pick up some stuff. We'll be right out."

The door to the family room banged open. Francesca's eyes swept over the room. They froze on the stained glass window behind Griff's head. "You cracked it?" Her voice shook.

Ganny ran and squeezed himself into the little space between the propped tree and the glass wall. Griff looked at the stained glass window. The crack was thin and curved like a spider's leg. He jumped off the couch. "We're sorry!" he said. "We'll pick everything up." His muscles tensed, waiting for Francesca to explode.

For a moment, all Griff could hear was his own breath and the clock ticking on the fireplace mantel.

Then, her mouth opened. But all that came out was a whisper. "My mom and I won first prize for that window."

She hunched her shoulders and began lifting photos off the floor.

Ganny emerged from behind the tree. The brothers looked at each other. They began working in silence, righting the lamp and pillows, returning bocce balls to the case.

When Francesca tried to right the tree, the boys helped. The three of them managed to restore it back to its upright position.

Ganny stepped on an ornament, crunching it underfoot.

From Francesca came a soft sound, like a kitten's mewl.

Outside a car horn blared.

"That's Mom!" Griff exclaimed. "She'll wake the baby!"

And sure enough, Guinevere began to shriek.

Francesca shuddered. She flung back her head, gripped her hair between both hands, and howled.

Griff stumbled back. Ganny covered his ears. "Stop stop stop!" he cried.

The baby's shrieks burned through the room. Francesca screamed, "Shut up, Guinevere! Just! Shut! Up!"

She collapsed into the rocking chair. Tears spilled. "I can't do this. I'm so tired. So cold." She bowed her head and began to rock, violently, back and forth.

Guinevere continued to cry—piercing, shuddering sobs.

Griff whispered to Ganny and left the room, closing the door behind him.

Francesca closed her eyes and covered her ears.

After a while, Francesca realized the baby's cries were easing. Suddenly, as though someone had turned off a radio, the cries stopped.

Francesca opened her eyes. She watched Gannon. He was picking ornaments off the floor and putting them back on the tree. He wasn't doing it right. He was adding too many ornaments to the same low branches.

"Gannon?"

He looked at the tree. "I didn't mean those peas looked like your eyes. They just look like eyes is what I meant. Anyone's eyes. Should I get you a blanket?"

"What?"

"Are you still cold? Should I get you a blanket?"

The door to the family room opened. Griff stood in the doorway. His mother, Lily, stood behind him. She was cradling Guinevere like a football in one arm, and propping a bottle in the baby's mouth with her other hand. On Guinevere's head was a knitted pink hat Francesca didn't recognize. Francesca had knitted most of Guinevere's hats, sweaters, and socks, too.

"She's beautiful," Lily said. "And what a marvelous set of lungs!" She stepped into the room.

Francesca stared at the hat. Nothing went on her daughter that Francesca didn't first wash.

"Griff told me they'd made a mess in here," Lily said. "And cracked your beautiful window. I'll get it fixed. Anyway, I thought the least I could do now was get Guinevere changed and fed for you. I found bottles in your fridge. I warmed one."

"She wasn't due for a bottle yet," Francesca said. "I'm trying to keep her on a schedule."

Lily nodded. She eased the bottle from Guinevere's mouth and handed it to Griff.

"She drank it all!" Griff exclaimed.

Lily lifted Guinevere to her shoulder and patted her back. A loud burp from the baby made the boys laugh. Despite her anger, Francesca smiled. Then she frowned. "That hat? Where'd it come from?"

Lily stepped closer. "I didn't know if it would fit. But it fits perfectly. I knitted it . . .a while ago."

Francesca felt dizzy. Had Lily knit the hat for her own baby girl? A sudden insight, sharp and painful, clicked inside her: Guinevere only existed because Grace did not.

"The hat, I'd thought I'd never finish it. There are heart shapes knit into the hat, and you had to follow the pattern perfectly to make the hearts. I kept making mistakes and had to start over."

"In knitting, there's no such thing as mistakes," Francesca heard herself say. "That's what my mother always said when I'd drop a stitch or purl when I should have knitted. A mistake, she'd say, is just the way a knitter personalizes her work."

Lily nodded. "That's a good philosophy. I wish I'd applied it to my own parenting when Griff was born. I was so by-the-book with him, I drove myself crazy. Then when Ganny came along, I was too tired and overwhelmed to even remember schedules and rules."

Francesca felt blood heat her face. What was Lily implying? That Francesca was too by-the-book?

"But," Lily continued, "I've got a rule-follower and a rule-breaker. So maybe I reaped what I sowed."

Francesca looked at the boys who were now sitting on the floor near the TV. The rule-follower. The rule-breaker. Which one would her daughter be? Which one was ultimately better to be? Which one would Grace have been?

Lily lowered her face to the baby nestled in her arms. She breathed deeply. "I'd forgotten how good a baby smells."

Francesca stood. The rocker nudged her knees, pushing her a step toward Lily. Lily looked tired. Purple stained the pouches under her eyes. Her brown hair looked dusty. But Guinevere, nestled against Lily, was gloriously quiet, content.

"Would you like a cup of coffee?" Francesca heard herself ask Lily. "Maybe a cappuccino?"

•

WHILE LILY ROCKED the baby, Francesca made cappuccino. She popped a big bowl of popcorn. She led the boys to the basement and let them bring up the two bean bag chairs Gary had bought without even asking her first.

The boys sat in the bean bag chairs and watched Nickelodeon, the sound low, the popcorn between them on the floor.

Francesca lay under a comforter on the couch. From half-opened eyes, she watched Lily rock Guinevere. She watched Lily's fingers trace the heart shapes on Guinevere's hat. The hat was adorable. Maybe she'd ask Lily for the pattern.

Francesca felt her stomach tighten. Was it Grace's hat? Had Grace ever worn it? Oh! The three Gs on the bocce balls. What an idiot she was. An insensitive idiot. Well, she would tell the boys that the third G was for *both* their sisters.

She looked at the boys cradled in the bean bag chairs. The chairs clashed with the décor, but Francesca had to admit that with the boys sitting in them, the chairs somehow looked right.

Griff suddenly turned and looked at her. She smiled, and when, this time, shockingly, he actually smiled back, she felt something bright and fierce sweep through her, swift, soft bristles scrubbing her clean.

Was it gladness? Grace?

The evening pressed darker and darker against the windows behind the tree. The lights on the tree began to pop out. Brighter and brighter they glowed, so that even after Francesca closed her eyes, she could feel their heat warming her skin.

Author's Note

Hockey great Wayne Gretzky famously said, "You miss 100% of the shots you don't take."

I don't play hockey. I don't follow hockey. I never even learned how to skate.

But Gretzky's affirmation is my mantra.

For writers, taking a shot is sending your work out. Scoring is when someone accepts your work, publishes it, and sometimes even pays you for it.

Over the past three decades, I've written 129 short stories. I've shot 82 of them across the cold expanse of ice toward that faraway, well-guarded net. I've scored only 27 times.

Ouch! Rejection always stings.

But of course, the only way to be sting-free in my writing life is never to send my work out, which then means never to experience the thrill of acceptance.

This book is the collection of my 27 stories that have previously been published. I wanted to gather them in one place, in a book I could hold in my hand and display—like a trophy—on my shelf.

I'm grateful for the assists from my family and writer friends who read and critiqued my story drafts. I'm grateful to the editors who published these stories, especially those who paid me.

And because you're holding this book and reading this note, I thank *you*.

Marie Anderson
La Grange, IL
February, 2017

Made in the USA
Lexington, KY
03 May 2017